"I am not a
in treating n

Amalie sat on the end of her bed staring at her reflection in the mirror on her nightstand and swiping at her eyes with the corner of the quilt. Papa would have her hide for sure, and the waiting only made it worse. She said the words again, reminding herself that she was indeed a full-grown woman who could make her own decisions. Somehow, though, the words hung in the thick bayou air; they didn't quite stick.

If only Papa hadn't caught her coming up the road toward home in the wee hours of the morning. With her suitcase in hand, explanations had not been necessary. It was plain what she'd originally been up to.

KATHLEEN MILLER Y'BARBO
is a tenth-generation Texan and mother of three grown sons and a teenaged daughter. She is a graduate of Texas A&M University and an award-winning novelist of Christian and young adult fiction. Kathleen is a former treasurer for the American Christian Fiction Writers and is a member of Inspirational Writers Alive, Words for the Journey, Writers Information Network, and The Writers Guild. Find out more about Kathleen at www. kathleenybarbo.com.

Books by Kathleen Miller Y'Barbo

HEARTSONG PRESENTS
HP474—You Can't Buy Love
HP529—Major League Dad
HP571—Bayou Fever
HP659—Bayou Beginnings
HP675—Bayou Secrets

Bayou Dreams

Kathleen Miller Y'Barbo

Heartsong Presents

To Rebecca Germany and Tracie Peterson, friends, blessings, and editors extraordinaire, and to Linda Mae Baldwin, a writer's researcher. Also, many thanks to Deb Kinnard for supplying the name of Tillie's diner. Without you, ladies, Amalie might still be waiting back in Latagnier for the bus—and her big break.

AUTHOR'S NOTE:

Acadian French is a spoken rather than written language, and much variation exists between it and modern French. Remember as you read this that I have attempted to give a bit of the flavor of early twentieth-century Louisiana and thus have incorporated some of the words and phrases used by Acadians of that time.

A note from the Author:
I love to hear from my readers! You may correspond with me by writing:

Kathleen Miller Y'Barbo
Author Relations
PO Box 721
Uhrichsville, OH 44683

ISBN 1-59310-937-7

BAYOU DREAMS

All scripture quotations are taken from the King James Version of the Bible.

Our mission is to publish and distribute inspirational products offering exceptional value and biblical encouragement to the masses.

PRINTED IN THE U.S.A.

one

"Papa, I'll be twenty-one soon, and you're still treating me like a child. In fact," Amalie Breaux added, "you gave me the same answer when I asked to go see *Gone With the Wind* two years ago."

Her father leaned away from the table, the chicory coffee still steaming in front of him. Mama was at the sink, her back to the room. The only hint she'd eavesdropped was the fact that she stood stock-still, dishwater dripping off elbows that had, only moments ago, been in motion.

Papa's copy of the *New Iberia Daily Leader* from last Sunday lay open before him with his well-worn Bible sitting atop it. In the margins of the book of James, Amalie could see scribblings in pencil and pen vying for attention among the words of the epistle, while on the margins of the paper he'd written a note to check the traps on the north end of the bayou tomorrow morning before he headed to town.

To the right of the pencil scratchings was an advertisement for *Prisoner of Dreams*, the next big movie out of Hollywood. Ever since she read the book, Amalie had played the story line in her head. Two men in love with the same mysterious and doomed woman. One stands trial for her murder but the other, well, what a story. Now that would be a movie; she just *had* to see it.

Never mind that Papa said a lady's disposition was too gentle to endure a thriller like *Prisoner*. Why, it couldn't be any more

5

stress-inducing than living in a houseful of brothers, sisters, aunts, and uncles. Besides, this was the debut performance of Mignon Dupree, the latest sensation to come from Europe. Her face had decorated more magazine covers than any other starlet last year. The rumor was she'd turned down contracts at all the big studios. Where she would do her next picture was a mystery.

Well, at least it used to be a mystery. Amalie hadn't read a screen magazine since before Christmas. Who knew what the lovely Miss Dupree was doing now? For all she knew, Mignon Dupree could be starring in the next *Gone with the Wind*.

If only Papa would relent. She just *had* to see *Prisoner of Dreams*.

The sound of their ancient Catahoula hound barking made her look up. Past the open back screen door that squealed and protested when used, the silly dog had treed another squirrel. Balanced with two big paws against the trunk of the sweet gum tree, his hind legs were securely grounded in the middle of Mama's Easter lily patch as his gray and brown tail cut a swath through the newly planted greenery.

Sure enough, her mother caught sight of the dog and went running, crossing the lawn with apron strings flying and a dish towel flapping in the stiff breeze. Shouting threats she had no intention of carrying out, she chastised the bewildered animal in rapid Acadian French. The dog did not seem to be bilingual at the moment, for he continued to bay at the fat treed squirrel.

"Get on, dog!" Amalie shouted as the dog slinked away. "Leave that squirrel be."

Papa lifted his dark brow and quirked his lips into a smile. When the dog had disappeared out of sight and Mama had begun reworking the damaged bed, Papa turned his attention back to Amalie. Before she could speak, he held up his hand to stop her.

"Now about this foolishness, eh? I said no two years ago

when you wanted to see that kind of movie, and you'll hear it again two years from now. Something with all that war and shooting is not suitable for girls your age, and besides. . ." Papa sipped at his coffee then gave a long-suffering sigh. "It would only cause you to start dreaming those silly dreams of yours again. Remember what happened the last year when I let your sisters take you to the picture show?" *Pride and Prejudice.* Amalie walked around for weeks afterward imitating Greer Garson and pretending she was rushing off to meet Lawrence Olivier in some idyllic spot. To be fair, it had driven her father to distraction to see her sashay about like a proper eighteenth-century lady and speak with diction that sounded like a foreign language to bayou folk.

He sighed again. "Amalie, I would give my life for you, *cher*, and you know it, eh?"

She knew where this line of questioning would go, but there was no denying the truth. "Yes, Papa. I know that."

"*Bien.*" He appeared to be deep in thought for a moment then abruptly swung his gaze to collide with hers. "*Ma fille,* I don't care how many times they show that movie, you are not going to New Iberia or anywhere else to see it." She watched him duck his head and reach for his pencil then touch the point to the beginning of the fourth chapter of James and start to underline. "*C'est fini,*" he said as he looked up at her.

Papa's eyes narrowed, and he seemed to dare her to look away. She did, unable to meet such a direct stare from one so revered and, at this moment, so reviled.

It's final? Well, of all the nerve. Obviously her father hadn't listened to a word she said.

Amalie stomped her feet and stormed away from the table, leaving Papa with the troubled expression she'd seen far too much of late. "All I'm asking is to see a movie that's been made from one of my favorite books," she called. "What's so awful about that?"

The familiar scrape of kitchen chair against wood floor brought her words and her steps to an abrupt halt. This time she'd really done it. She whirled around to see if Papa had followed.

Swallowing the apology she knew she should make, Amalie squared her shoulders and waited. Maybe Papa had finally listened. Maybe he *had* given some thought to the fact that she was a grown woman, a woman with thoughts and plans for her life. Thankful her interest in acting had taught her to control her emotions, Amalie adjusted her worried look to force a nervous smile.

What would Greer Garson or Mignon Dupree have done had either invoked the ire of her father? Amalie contemplated this, but nothing came to mind. No relative of the refined Miss Garson or the mysterious Miss Dupree could be anything like Papa.

Still she waited. Why did Papa choose this particular morning to move so slowly? Generally her father, though a large man, walked with a quick purposeful stride, only slowing down to match the pace of Mama or one of his ten children.

And yet today he obviously felt no need to hurry.

Any hope that her speech had been effective vanished when Papa, coffee cup in hand, walked past her without comment. As he pushed open the screen door and disappeared outside, Amalie closed her eyes and sighed. Along with regret, the scent of Mama's strong chicory coffee swirled around her.

"You know you catch more flies with honey than you do with vinegar, *cher*. Your papa, he's set in his ways, but you know he loves you, eh?"

Amalie opened her eyes to see Mama standing in the doorway wiping her hands with the corner of her apron. When their gazes met, Mama shook her head then smiled.

"Yes, I know he acts like this because he loves me." She paused to draw in a long breath and exhale dramatically. "But he's impossible, Mama. He's stubborn and set in his ways and can't see that anyone else might have a valid opinion. Honestly, I don't see how you live with the man."

Mama chuckled and motioned for Amalie to follow her back into the kitchen. "Oh, honey, if you only knew how much you're like him."

"I am not," she insisted, even as she considered the truth of the statement.

Certainly she did have her opinion about things, and any intelligent person would see that hers was generally the correct one, but no one would call her stubborn or set in her ways. At least no one with any discernment.

Besides, this time Papa was just plain wrong, and that's all there was to it.

"Mama, you know how I love going to the movies. On top of that, I've read and reread *Prisoner of Dreams* until the pages are falling out of it. It's just a *movie*," she repeated for effect, this time adding a dramatic sigh. "Papa's acting like I want to run off with the circus."

Mama lifted one dark brow but said nothing.

"What?"

Again her mother shook her head. "You go on talking, *bebe*. I do love to listen to my girl when she's on her soapbox."

"I'm not on my soapbox. I'm just stating a fact. Your *husband* is treating me like a child. I will be twenty-one soon."

"You will be twenty-one the fourteenth of May, Amalie Breaux. That's two months away, and I'll thank you not to rush it. Also, as long as you draw a breath, you will be my *bebe*. I feel that way about all of my children, and I 'spect Papa feels the same." She paused to wave away Amalie's objection. "Now as for that speech you're in the middle of, let me know when you're done, and maybe you and me can figure out a way to get your papa to see another side of the situation, eh?"

"You'd help me change Papa's mind?"

"I might." Mama grinned. "If I knew you were going with a suitable escort."

Amalie named several friends from church who were expecting to attend with her. To her surprise, Mama frowned then shook her head.

"That's not what I meant," she said. "And I doubt Papa will care if your friends are going. You need an adult. A parent, maybe."

A parent? Hadn't Mama heard a thing Amalie said? Did she not see a maturity level that far surpassed her brothers and, for that matter, her sisters as well? And didn't she remember that by this age her sister Mathilde had already given birth to Teddy and her sister-in-law Genevieve was raising baby Ellen *and* holding down a full-time job?

And forget the fact that Mama had been married to Papa long enough to have two babies before she was twenty-one.

"You know, Amalie," Mama said as she rubbed a speck of dust off the door facing with the corner of her apron, "I always did think that Mr. Stu Stevens was a handsome man."

She gave Mama a sideways look. "Mama, I don't believe I've ever heard you refer to anyone but Papa like that."

"Well, he looks a bit like your papa, don't you think? That wavy dark hair and those eyes. . ." Mama giggled as she touched Amalie's hand. "You leave your papa to me. Just stay out of his way, and, above all, keep your thoughts to yourself. Can you do that?"

"I'll do my best." She paused to shake her head. "But, Mama, how are you going to change Papa's mind? I mean, he is the very definition of stubborn."

Again Mama giggled. "You leave that to me. Just stay out of his way and don't cross him, eh?"

two

Tuesday, March 18

While her brother Ernest and his wife, Genevieve, took care of the little ones, Mama got to see those eyes and the rest of Mr. Stevens, Miss Mignon Dupree, and the entire cast of *Prisoner of Dreams* at the afternoon matinee. Rather than accompany them, Papa elected to take the afternoon to catch up with his buddies at the feed store and then have the tires replaced on the Ford.

Going to a movie alone with Mama was the treat of a lifetime for Amalie. Born sixth out of ten children, she was more used to sharing her mother than having her to herself. When she settled beside Mama in the next to last row of the Evangeline Theater, she said a prayer of thanks for getting to be with her.

By the time Papa drove up to the theater to fetch them, Amalie had made a decision. She would someday grace the big screen just like Mignon Dupree.

After all, why would the Lord give her a talent if He didn't intend for her to use it? And didn't everyone rave over her performance in the church Christmas play? Why, it was a natural expectation that someone who was given the ability should be pursuing the stage.

Surely the Lord would expect nothing less from her.

Amalie had been saving her egg money for nearly a year in the hopes of sending off for the acting course she'd read about in the screen magazines. Now she would alter that purpose and consider her savings as the means to get to California

11

and her destiny. Surely she had no need of a course. When the producers out there got wind of her talent, they would be fighting each other to hire her.

"So what did you think of the movie, Cleo?" Papa asked Mama.

Mama slid Amalie a sideways look. "Oh, I liked it well enough." She winked at Amalie. "Theo, did anyone ever tell you how much you look like that handsome Mr. Stevens?"

Amalie grinned as Papa shook his head and signaled to turn onto the road leading toward Latagnier. "I wonder what it would be like to be a real movie actor," she said.

"Now that's exactly what I was afraid of, Cleo. But do I listen to myself? No, I listen to the womenfolk, and what happens, eh?"

He slowed his speed to fall in behind a truck carrying a load of chickens. Amalie covered her nose with her handkerchief and tried not to look at the poor caged birds. Their plight and hers seemed far too similar.

"Oh, Theo," Mama said, "you're making too much of this. Our *bebe*, she's just a little starstruck, that's all." She patted his shoulder. "You and I both know she doesn't *really* want to be a movie actress. Why, there's not a girl born on the bayou who could expect to—"

"But I do, Mama. I want to be just like Mignon Dupree." The words were out before she realized she'd spoken them. The damage done, Amalie plowed forward. "Why, I already have her dark hair and eyes, and I can change my voice to suit the role just like she does. She's really French, you know."

She paused to stare at her stunned mother then cast a quick glance at the back of her father's head. Neither spoke. A good sign.

"Whether you agree or not, I am no longer a child, and I intend to go to California someday very soon."

Papa stomped hard on the brakes, nearly sending Amalie

onto the floorboards. He turned to glower in her direction. "There will be no more talk of movies and such. Pure nonsense, it is. I'll not have a daughter of mine flaunting herself like those movie people. I love you, baby girl, and I want you right here where you belong. Among bayou folks."

Indignation rose. "Papa, that's not fair."

Her father barely blinked. She didn't dare look at Mama. Time to take another angle.

"I love you, too, Papa, and I can see your point, but I've prayed over this, and I feel that God is leading me to the stage."

Where she expected a softened expression, anger showed. "Daughter, do not dare speak of the Lord in such a casual way. Yes, He leads, but toward godly endeavors. I dare you to tell me how one soul will be saved or one starving child will be fed by you prancing around in front of a movie camera pretending to be someone you're not."

She had to think hard to come up with an answer, but finally a suitable one surfaced. "Acting in the movies could very well be where my ministry is. Are you saying you want to deny me that?"

"Isn't that funny?" Papa said slowly. "It sounds like you're not so worried about what you can do for the Lord as you are worried about what this supposed ministry will do for you."

"That's not true." But was it? The jolt in her heart told her she couldn't be sure.

Papa glanced at Mama then turned back toward Amalie. "Those movie magazines you buy—that's what's causing this foolishness. I don't mind you reading good books, and I'm not even bothered by the ladies' magazines your mama has lying about." He paused to let out a long breath. "But, Amalie Breaux, you are taking all this movie business too far. If you want to find a life's calling, don't go to the screen books—go to the Good Book. The Bible's got what you need."

"I read the Bible, too," she protested. "And the Bible says 'Where there is no vision the people perish.' Proverbs 29, eighteenth verse. Papa, I truly believe my vision is to act in the movies. Please know I'm not trying to hurt you. I'm just trying to follow my dreams. If you make me stay here in Latagnier, I will surely perish."

He shook his head. "I don't know what else to say. I love you, Amalie, and I don't aim to let you make a mistake you'll regret."

She opened her mouth to speak, but his look silenced her. Instead she pleaded silently with Mama to intervene, knowing the odds were not in her favor. Mama frowned, her alliance chosen.

Of course Mama would side with Papa. She always did. Well, most of the time anyway.

"Now forget about this nonsense," Papa said. "Set your sights on something else. Say, what about the Dautrive boy? He's been coming around a lot lately. Maybe it's time to start thinking about marrying up with someone."

Timothy Dautrive? The preacher's son?

The thought of spending an hour with him gave her the willies, much less pledging a lifetime. Sure, he'd been coming around some, but more to eat up Mama's vittles than to court. Why, the poor fellow was so tongue-tied he couldn't even discuss the weather without blushing. He sure could put away the gumbo and pie, though.

At this rate he'd go from sturdy to stout in no time.

"But, Papa, I—"

"Don't you 'But, Papa' me, young lady. I better never catch you with another one of those magazines, or there'll be more trouble than you know what to do with. You hear me, *cher*?"

Her mouth said, "Yes, Papa," but her heart said the opposite.

The ride back to Latagnier was the longest of her life. With every mile that slipped past, Amalie's spirits sank.

Why hadn't she been born somewhere besides here? To grow up Acadian had its merits for some, but for Amalie the close-knit society and overlarge family felt more like a burden than a blessing.

આ

March somehow turned to April and then to May, the days passing without fanfare. Other than a lovely Easter cantata where she was blessed with a solo performance, Amalie had no outlet for her theatrical ambitions.

Her May birthday arrived and as quickly was gone; then came the heat of summer. As stifling June days and lazy July afternoons passed in endless and unchanging succession, dreams of movie stardom made Amalie's dreary bayou life tolerable. The growing pile of money in the sock gave her hope—and a plan to end this madness before she became chained to the crib and diaper pail like her older sisters.

Papa must have sensed her dispirited attitude, for he finally came around the outdoor kitchen one early August morning to stand against an old fence post and watch her work. He said nothing, and neither did she, until they both broke the silence at once.

"You go first, Papa," Amalie said.

Papa cleared his throat. "All right, I will," he said as he studied the tips of his callused fingers. "I was thinking I might head on into town in a bit." He swung his gaze up to meet hers. "You want to come along, eh?"

Amalie's breath caught. Part of her banishment from all things related to stage and theater was to forgo most of the trips Papa made to New Iberia.

It wasn't that he told her she couldn't go. He simply didn't invite her. For her part, Amalie would have refused if he had. It had taken him until the second day of August to swallow his pride.

It shamed her that Papa made the first move.

Before she could respond, Papa shrugged and turned away. "Well, maybe another time," he said as he headed toward the barn where the Ford awaited.

For a heartbeat she watched him go, wanting desperately to punish him for laying waste to her dreams. Instead she found herself trotting to catch up then lacing her fingers in his without a word.

They rode all the way to town like that, keeping their silence and forging a quiet peace on tender ground. In New Iberia, Papa let her off at the five-and-dime before turning the Ford in the direction of the feed store. He'd be there awhile, Amalie knew, so she ducked inside the store and headed for the magazine section.

There it was: *Movie Stars Parade*, with Judy Garland on the cover. Beside it sat *Screen Scene*, the announcement of a newly formed movie studio vying for attention with a headline announcing Greer Garson's new gazebo and pool house.

Then she saw it: *Hollywood Journal, Special Edition*. And there on the cover, dressed for the summer in a frock of brilliant red, was Mignon Dupree. The headline beneath the photo stated that she'd signed a contract for her next movie. "Details inside."

Well, Amalie had to have that issue along with the other two. Papa would have her hide if he knew what she bought, but to her mind there was nothing wrong with magazines that gave a glimpse into the glamorous life of movie actors. Still, she rolled the precious purchases into a manageable size and tucked them into her handbag. Tonight she would read by the light of her flashlight, keeping the covers tucked firmly around her despite the stifling heat.

She marched to the soda fountain and ordered a cherry lemonade then sipped it slowly and let her mind travel west to the movie lot where cameras whirred and directors shouted things like "action" and "cut." Eyes closed, she let the sour sweet liquid slide down the back of her throat while she imagined herself to be Greer Garson taking a sip of lemonade under the cooling shade of her new gazebo. Another sip and she'd become the doomed ingénue from *Prisoner of Dreams*; a third and she danced in the Busby Berkley chorus.

Mindful of her imaginary feather-plumed hat, Amalie set the glass on the counter and rested her elbows on either side. A sigh escaped her lips as she reached for the fan she kept in her purse. Bright blue with Tillman's Mortuary emblazoned on either side, the fan kicked up a small and welcome breeze.

The ice cubes clinked and settled lower in the glass as Amalie shouldered her purse. She really should stroll down to the feed store and meet Papa. He'd be ready to go soon—that is, if Ziggy Labauve, part-time taxidermist and owner of the feed store, hadn't launched into one of his many colorful stories about the First World War. Once that happened, a body could only sit and wait for him to come up for air.

The magazine in her purse called to her, and she lifted her purse onto the counter. What would it hurt to take a little peek at the newest issue? After all, this was a special edition, not just the run-of-the-mill screen magazine.

Amalie cast a furtive glance toward the door then leaned forward to stare out the window that faced the feed store. The Ford still sat out front, and Papa was nowhere to be seen.

Just one peek. The feature story was on Mignon Dupree after all. Then there was the other magazine. A new studio meant new movies and, possibly, openings for new starlets to act in those movies.

That's right, she decided as she lifted the magazine out of her purse and settled it across her lap. *Just one peek.* She flipped to the story in question and began to read, looking up toward the feed store and the Ford every few minutes.

It seemed as though an Italian director and some of his friends were on the verge of creating the latest greatest thing with their new Civil War movie. Rumors surrounded the new picture now being cast.

The only sure information the magazine could confirm was that meetings had been held at an undisclosed location, the result of which was a movie deal with Mignon Dupree. There was even talk that the great silent film star Charlotte Crawford, who had played a cameo role in her husband's movie *Prisoner of Dreams*, might once again come out of retirement to take a costarring role.

A twenty-year-old photograph of Miss Crawford sipping lemonade poolside with Mary Pickford and Douglas Fairbanks at Pickfair decorated one part of the page while a larger shot of her holding her infant son bore the caption, "Motherhood has given me what films could not: happiness. I thank God for bringing me Roberto and our son." A more recent photograph of the actress, flanked by a swarthy Italian gentleman and a handsome young man in a graduation gown from the Citadel, proclaimed her to be happy in her retirement with her husband and pilot son and serving God as a patron to missions around the world. The article went on to note that her passions were gardening and awaiting the future arrival of grandchildren.

"Well, now, isn't that something?" Amalie whispered. What must it be like to be Charlotte Crawford? To give up a career for home and family and digging in flower beds? "Could I do that?"

"Amalie Breaux, get to the car right now before I make you walk back to Latagnier."

She scrambled off the stool and found her footing just as Papa reached for her elbow. "Papa," she said as she kicked the magazine out of sight with the toe of her shoe, "you scared me to death."

For a moment her father stood and glared. Then his gaze dropped to the ground and the magazine only inches from her foot. Reaching to retrieve it, he shook the offending periodical in her direction.

"This is yours."

Not a question but a statement. The only thing Amalie was left to wonder was whether she heard anger or sorrow in her father's voice. One look at his face, and she knew which one.

Papa was furious.

"The car," he said. "Go now. We can discuss this at home."

"I don't want to talk about this, Papa." Amalie straightened her spine and stared into the eyes of the man who loved her and intended to ruin her life all at the same time. "And as to going home, what if I would rather go to the bus station instead?"

Time stopped, and it seemed as though the very breath went out of Papa. Then, without a word, he turned on his heel and strode outside.

He expected her to follow him, and she did. Not because she wanted to, but because she'd unwisely left her egg money in the sock under her mattress.

Not a word was exchanged on the long drive home, and when Papa pulled up the Ford in front of the house he climbed out and stalked inside. Amalie ignored her mother's questioning glance to snatch up the egg basket and head for the henhouse.

The rest of the evening, Amalie made it her business to keep out of Papa's way, even turning down Mama's roast and potatoes for a cold sandwich eaten on the sly.

The next day was Sunday, so Amalie bided her time. Walking through the motions of church and Sunday dinner was awful. She felt like a rag doll propped up first in a church pew and then at her usual place at the dinner table.

Sunday night Amalie climbed into bed early, pleading exhaustion from the heat. Once the house settled and the night fell hard, she climbed out of bed and walked all the way to town to be the first in line when the bus pulled out of the station Monday morning.

three

Europe might be in the throes of war, but at the Tratelli household the only hint of discord was in the pudding—the Welsh pudding. It seemed as though the oven had a problem, and luncheon guests were waiting on a main course that had yet to be cooked.

Roberto Antonio Lamonica Tratelli III leaned against his pop's favorite Silver Shadow, parked conveniently near the back door—and the rear exit of the property—and watched Cook give orders in her familiar Jamaican lilt. Shortly afterward, Cook had steaks sizzling on the spit and her special sauce bubbling on the stove.

Heads would roll over the runny pudding—figuratively, of course. Then, when things calmed down, Cook would get a raise. Mother presided over the dining table—now moved outside in the shade of the eucalyptus grove—while Pop seemed to be snoozing in his overlarge chair on the opposite end. A dozen executives from the newly formed Imperial Studio held court between the pair, interspersed between wives and the occasional girlfriend, and none of them seemed to notice the delay or the fact that their host was snoring.

The topic of choice today, as it had been since the first of August, was Senate Resolution 152. While Rob steered clear of any topic related to movies, he did find it fascinating that the government was worried about film folks inciting people to go to war. With hearings set for the fall, much discussion would take place in regard to the issue. And certainly many more lunches like this one.

Rob straightened his shoulders and tugged at the tourniquet his father called appropriate neckwear. Were it not for the endless parade of occasions to wear the detested thing, he might not mind. Ah, but Casa Tratelli, situated on a coveted piece of Brentwood Canyon real estate, was *the* place for movie folks to be seen.

Rob chuckled as he recalled overhearing a recent conversation between his parents. While his mother tried to explain the logic of having a pool house built for the convenience of guests at an upcoming charity event, his father attempted to sneak in an opinion or two as to the absurdity of such an expense.

"Why don't you give the money to the church building fund and be done with it, *bella*?" Pop's exasperated sigh punctuated the statement.

"Well, isn't that the silliest thing I've ever heard? Robbie, darling, did you hear your father? Surely he can see that if we spend a little now, the end result will be a much higher donation. Besides, a pool house will give us another place to offer to those dear folks doing missions work. I would certainly hate to meet the Lord when my time comes and have to explain why I didn't do my part."

"Yes, dear." Pop's favorite answer when he had no answer.

"Honey lamb," his mother said in her throaty South Carolina drawl, "don't you realize our home is *the* place for movie folks to see and be seen? Where else are they going to get a little entertainment and a whole lot of the gospel?"

With Pop's last two movies doing blockbuster business and the next production currently in casting over at Imperial, Rob doubted his father needed to open his home to strangers and business acquaintances to make a buck. He did, however, love to take any opportunity to wax poetic on his Lord and Savior.

In typical Tratelli style, Pop managed never to offend or preach, but he always got the Lord's message across. Mother said if Pop hadn't made a success of the movie business, he would have become a missionary. The end result of his parents' conversation that day had been that Mother got her second pool house and Pop got a small slice of peace and quiet—or at least that was the theory.

In reality, Casa Tratelli had no peace and quiet. The place bustled with a rotating guest list of directors, producers, screenwriters, actors, financial bigwigs with too much money and not enough good sense when it came to the movie business, and—most important—missionaries.

The end result was an interesting mix of Hollywood and the heaven-bound. Pop loved them all equally, cultivating friendships that took him from Beverly Hills to Houston, from New York and—before the war—overseas to England and his native Italy.

With conflict raging across Europe, Pop had long ago sent for his siblings and their relatives, giving all who responded jobs in the movie business—from janitor to general manager. In the two years since emigrating, cousin Gregorio had achieved moderate success writing scripts. Uncle Marco Cantoni, an accomplished violinist and former symphony director in his native Florence as well as husband to Pop's late sister, had tested the waters in writing movie scores with mixed success. Uncle Marco's son Benny, however, landed a job in management at Central Casting while Benny's twin brother, Eduardo, walked away from his training as a classical Shakespearean actor to flip burgers as a fry cook at the Starlight Grill, a burger joint in the shadows of the Paramount lot.

Then there was Helena.

Daughter of Pop's youngest brother, Giovanni, Helena had been Rob's only friend growing up—a poverty-stricken girl sent to America to keep her cousin company. Back when the whole family—Mother, Pop, and occasionally a nanny— traveled to movie locations, Helena was his sole companion and partner-in-crime.

When the pair hit their teens and Mama put her foot down against the nomadic life, the four of them settled in Brentwood, making their home in a eucalyptus grove nestled against a canyon wall and safe from the changing world of movies and film.

Or so it was intended.

Through the stability of a "normal life" and the structure of classes at Hollywood High, Rob found contentment. With regular church attendance came a renewed faith in God.

Helena, however, bristled at the regularity of things, often complaining bitterly at having to give up the exciting life of a world traveler. Soon, however, she found her excitement elsewhere, in the lure of the darker side of Hollywood.

What happened to Helena was a large part of the reason Rob detested the whole industry. No girl should end up as his beloved cousin had, and yet so many did.

Rob was thankful Helena's father, Uncle Giovanni, came to stay not long after Helena's death. Uncle Gio was an airman, one of those rare fellows who would rather fly than almost anything else. For the past three years Rob had spent countless hours at the airpark with Uncle Gio cultivating a love of flying that Rob intended to turn into a career.

A career that had nothing to do with the movie business.

"Oh, look, there's the birthday boy."

A pair of Veronica Lake look-alikes strolled toward him, arms linked and smiles turned up to identical wattages. Rob tried not to cringe.

"Hello, handsome." The taller one broke ranks with her companion and sidled up next to him. "You're the director's son, aren't you?"

The director's son.

With a skill honed over the years, Ron kept a neutral expression. The Maker's son? Now that was a relationship worth owning up to—one his mother made sure he cultivated with regularity. "The director's son," however, hit him wrong every time he heard it.

He was proud of Pop and all. Who wouldn't be? Everything the man touched turned to movie gold. And who could ask for a better, godlier father?

To those unschooled in Bible lore, his current hit was just another Hollywood epic. But to Rob and the others who understood the story told in the book of Ruth, *Prisoner of Dreams* held a much deeper meaning. But then Pop managed to get a bit of Truth in everything he did.

Rob looked past the women to the south, where the city of Los Angeles beckoned. By dusk another set of partygoers would arrive and the process of entertaining Hollywood glitterati would begin again.

"Cat got your tongue, sweetheart?" This from Blond Number One. "C'mon and say something. After all, a little bird told me today's a special day for you."

A little bird? More like the embarrassing arch over the driveway, courtesy of the Paramount prop department, replete with balloons, streamers, and his name in ten-foot letters beneath a sign that read "OUR BOY'S TWENTY-FIVE." How he hated his birthday.

Blond Number Two attached herself to his arm with fingers finished off in blood-red nails. "You mean he's Roberto Tratelli's kid?"

Rob offered both ladies a practiced smile as he extricated himself from their grasp. "It's been a pleasure, ladies," he said as he made good his escape and slipped past the Silver Shadow and through a familiar break in the hibiscus that lined the path. Emerging on the other side of the hedge, he picked his way twenty yards down-canyon to a rocky outcropping that had become his prayer place.

The sun beat down on the valley and set rocks shimmering. Here against the sheltered wall of the canyon, the air held a cool freshness. Rob inhaled until his lungs protested then exhaled on a long breath.

So many people aspired to his life—or rather to what they imagined his life to be.

Lord, just once I wish I could be known as my own person and not some version of my father. Or worse, as some means to reach Pop to land a spot in a movie. Isn't there anyplace I can go where I'm simply Your child?

A hand clamped down on his shoulder, and he jumped, nearly vaulting headfirst into the canyon below. "Hey, there, cousin," Eduardo Cantoni said. "Did I scare you?"

Rob straightened and forced his breathing into something resembling normal then stared back at his cousin, eyes narrowed. "Nah, what made you think that?"

Ed chuckled as he reached to shake Rob's hand. "Really, I'm sorry, Rob-o. I just came by to wish you a happy birthday. I figured I'd look here first."

"Thanks." Rob settled back into his spot and motioned for Ed to take a seat beside him. "But the party's back at the house."

"I'll bet. Bunch of suits from back East?"

"Not this time," Rob said. "The Imperial folks."

"That would have been my second guess." His cousin pressed a small paper sack toward Rob. "This is from Tillie," he said with a grin.

Tillie Rush was a character no Hollywood screenwriter could create. The ageless red-haired matron had taken a liking to Rob the first time he wandered in to her establishment to visit his cousin. A running joke had developed between the two of them: Someday Rob would work for her at the

Starlight Grill, and she would retire to write her memoirs.

Given what little Rob knew of Tillie's escapades in early Hollywood, a number of studio executives no doubt quaked in their loafers over the prospect of Tillie telling all. But she had given her life and her energies to the Lord some quarter of a century ago, bringing a halt to several decades of wild living.

He opened the bag to find a cupcake, iced in chocolate and sprinkled with multicolored edible confetti. Atop the confection was a single candle. In the bottom of the bag he found a book of matches taped to a folded napkin.

"Make a wish," he read. Rob swung his gaze toward Ed. "She's too much."

"Yeah, she's a special gal. She sure has taken to you." Ed reached for the matches and lit the candle. "All right now, make a wish."

"You're kidding, right?"

Ed affected a serious look. "Do you honestly expect me to go back to the Starlight Grill and report to Tillie that you did *not* make a wish as she requested?"

Rob smiled. "I see your point. All right. Hand me that cupcake."

He searched his brain for something that might pass as an acceptable wish for Tillie. Somehow wishing for his dream of owning an aviation business seemed silly, perhaps because of the enormity of the dream.

"You're going to set the icing on fire," Ed said. "Make a wish already."

"Give me a minute. Wait. I've got it." *For once I'd like to be anonymous—plain old Rob and not Rob-the-son-of-the-famous-director.* He inhaled and quickly extinguished the candle then glanced at Ed, who gave him an expectant look.

"Well?" Ed asked. "What did you wish for?"

"Something that will never happen."

four

"I am *not* a child, and Papa is absolutely wrong in treating me like one."

Amalie sat on the end of her bed staring at her reflection in the mirror on her nightstand and swiping at her eyes with the corner of the quilt. Papa would have her hide for sure, and the waiting only made it worse. She said the words again, reminding herself that she was indeed a full-grown woman who could make her own decisions. Somehow, though the words hung in the thick bayou air, they didn't quite stick.

If only Papa hadn't caught her coming up the road toward home in the wee hours of the morning. With her suitcase in hand, explanations had not been necessary. It was plain what she'd originally been up to.

Papa should have been happy she didn't go through with her plan to leave on the first bus out of New Iberia. Instead he'd said not a word, choosing to confiscate her suitcase and point toward the house with a solemn face rather than offer her a ride home.

She'd walked for the better part of an hour with Papa following a distance behind in the Ford. Once she reached the house and stepped inside, he'd sped off like the devil himself was in pursuit.

Now, as the first rays of the sun announced a new day, Amalie couldn't help but wonder if the bus she'd intended

27

to be on was now idling in front of the station. If she hadn't forgotten her Bible, she'd be sitting on that bus headed for Shreveport, Dallas, and eventually Hollywood.

Amalie reached for the cause of her discomfort—and her comfort—and let the Bible fall open to the fourth chapter of the book of Galatians.

"Now I say, That the heir, as long as he is a child, differeth nothing from a servant, though he be lord of all; but is under tutors and governors until the time appointed of the father. Even so we, when we were children, were in bondage under the elements of the world."

Amalie paused to wipe her eyes. Yes, she knew all about being a child in bondage. Why, that certainly described her current situation. She turned her gaze back to the book she held in her shaking hand.

"But when the fullness of the time was come, God sent forth his Son, made of a woman, made under the law, to redeem them that were under the law, that we might receive the adoption of sons. And because ye are sons, God hath sent forth the Spirit of his Son into your hearts, crying, Abba, Father. Wherefore thou art no more a servant, but a son; and if a son, then an heir of God through Christ."

Closing the Bible, she set it back on the nightstand. "I'm an heir, not a servant," she whispered. "Why can't Papa see that?"

"Why can't Papa see what?"

She looked up to see her father standing in the doorway. Silhouetted by the growing light, he looked at once menacing and comforting. Under different circumstances she might have run to him and settled into an embrace guaranteed to cure whatever ailed her.

But today Papa was what ailed her. And the cure was not in his hands, but rather idling in front of the New Iberia bus station.

The object of her thoughts moved away from the door to settle his large frame on the other end of the narrow bed. His face wore lines she was certain were not there last night.

"Amalie," he said softly as he studied the veins on the back of his hand, "a papa's job, it's hard, eh? The Lord, He gives this duty to a man well before that man is prepared." He swung his gaze to meet Amalie's. "But that's the nature of things. The Father, He trusts that a man will do his best to raise the babies he's given. I take that trust seriously, *ma fille*."

"I know," she managed through trembling lips.

"When I was a young man, about your age, I believed there was nothing for me here on the bayou. I was convinced the Lord had a purpose for me and it was up north, Canada maybe." He shrugged. "Anywhere but Latagnier."

This revelation silenced the protest Amalie had ready.

Papa reached across the space between them to take her hand. Amalie saw the scars and calluses, a workingman's hand, and felt her heart swell with warmth. She also felt shame rise. Despite his faults, chief among them stubbornness and an inability to see Amalie as an adult, Papa was a good man and an even better father.

"Please know that I love you when I tell you this," Papa said with difficulty. "I've been speaking to the pastor."

The warmth in her heart faded to a chill. "About me?"

"Yes," Papa said.

Silence hung in the air. Whatever he had to say must have slowed Papa considerably. By now her usually demonstrative father would have spoken his piece, dealt out his punishment, and left to do the next chore on his considerable list. The fact he'd sat here this long without saying what he came to say did not bode well.

Papa abruptly released his grip and stood. He made it all the way to the door before turning to stare in her direction. "You can sit here all day, Amalie. I don't want you leaving this room until I decide what to do with you."

Amalie returned his stare, stunned.

"But, Papa, I—" The look he gave her chased her complaint away. She gathered her wits and her acting skills to redirect her frown into a smile. "Papa," she said sweetly, "thank you for giving me the time to think about what I've done, but truly I don't need it." She moved toward him across the small room, linking her arm with his to look up into his eyes. "I'm sorry, Papa—really I am."

She wasn't, and somewhere deep inside a nagging voice complained at her deceit. There would be plenty of time to make things right with Papa. Once she arrived in California, she would write to tell him so. In the meantime, she had to take on the greatest acting challenge of her life: assuming the role of the contrite daughter.

"I've learned my lesson, Papa—really I have," she said as she crossed her fingers behind her back.

Papa seemed to believe her for a moment. Then his expression turned to stone. He looked past her, and Amalie quickly uncrossed her fingers and turned to see what he found so upsetting.

The mirror.

"Cross your fingers, will you?" Papa's voice thundered and echoed in the tiny room. "Do you think the heavenly Father cannot see, even if I had not?"

Her "No, sir" was timid at best.

"Then you stay right here and think about what He must be thinking of you now. Defying your papa and breaking your mama's heart, indeed. Don't you leave this room, you hear?"

He whirled and stormed away, disappearing down the hall. The sound of his footsteps echoed in the room and in Amalie's heart. Never had she and Papa tangled for this long. If she didn't know better, she would think her designs on stardom had changed their once-close relationship. That couldn't be, of course, for the path God had set her on couldn't possibly lead her away from her parents.

Or could it?

The realization dawned that she might have to choose between what Papa wanted for her and what her heavenly Father intended.

"Where are you going?" Amalie heard Mama call to Papa.

"To fetch something that will take care of this problem with Amalie once and for all."

"The girl's too old to take a switch to, Theo," Mama said.

"That's not what I intend." The windows rattled as Papa slammed the door.

Amalie rushed to the window to see her father's long strides take him across the lawn and beyond to disappear into his workshop, her suitcase in his hand. She sank back onto her bed and sighed.

Now what?

A few minutes later the door slammed again, and Papa's footsteps headed her way. Too soon he stood in her doorway.

"Amalie Breaux, I love you, and you know it. The good Lord, He knows it, too." He shifted positions, one hand on the door frame and the other behind his back. "And your mama and me, we been praying He would fix whatever it is in you that makes you talk foolishness and act like you don't belong here with us."

She swallowed hard but said nothing.

The expression on Papa's face went from fierce to something very near defeat. If he were an actor on the stage, she would have been impressed with his ability to convey such a range of emotions. Instead she felt only shame.

Well, shame mixed with a healthy amount of indignation. How dare Papa decide what the Lord wanted for her?

"Daughter, you've disappointed your mama and me, and you

tried to run off to who-knows-where to boot." He shrugged. "I hate that I have to do this, but it's for your own good. Your mama'll bring you some lunch after a while. I don't 'spect you deserve breakfast. Come supper, I hope to have decided what to do with you."

The door slammed, and silence reigned.

"I set the dog out under your window, so don't think one of us won't hear it if you try to get out," he added from somewhere down the hall.

The day wore on in an endless chain of hours spent alternately combing the pages of her Bible and wrestling with her conscience and her plans. At half past twelve, Mama arrived with a plate, and twenty minutes later she returned to retrieve it.

Neither time did she speak or, for that matter, make eye contact. She was too heartbroken to make the attempt. Mama, it seemed, merely had nothing to say.

Somehow Amalie made it through the afternoon and the long evening when the darkness closed in and lamplight filled her room. No one came to bring supper, nor did they seem to miss her at what sounded like a lively table filled with family. By bedtime her stomach growled, and her mind churned.

As the house settled into quiet slumber, a soft knock came at the door. Before Amalie could respond, Mama—in her nightdress, her hair braided in a rope that fell past her waist—pushed the door open and set a tray with a glass of milk, cheese, and bread on the nightstand. She turned to leave without sparing Amalie a glimpse.

"Mama," she whispered.

Her mother stopped to glance over her shoulder. "*Oui?*"

A half dozen statements danced on her tongue. She ignored them all to state simply, "*Je t'aime, Maman.*"

Mama looked as if she might cry as she reached for the

doorknob. "I love you, too, *ma fille*."

"Mama, do you believe what Papa's doing is right?"

Her mother seemed to consider the question before shaking her head. "What matters is that I believe what you did was wrong. Theo, he's handling this as best as he knows how. Me, I don't know what I would do with you, and that's the honest truth."

She crossed the small space to kiss the top of Amalie's head.

"Don't go," Amalie said quickly.

Mama turned and swiped at her eyes with the backs of her hands. "I can't stay, Amalie, not with Papa in such a mood."

She watched her mother's back disappear into the hallway. A moment later the door shut with a soft click.

"Me either, Mama."

Amalie reached for her pillowcase to stuff it full, starting with her Bible. This time there would be no coming back. This time she would make it all the way to California.

To Hollywood.

She raised the sash on the window to peer outside. The hound dog Papa perceived as a threat lay snoring happily. Mama's old orange cat stretched and switched her tail then pranced off.

Her conscience told her to go to bed and hope for a better day tomorrow, but her pride spoke louder, urging her to try the escape she'd planned all afternoon. After all, she deserved her shot at fame. Papa would thank her when the money she made from acting in the movies bought him a new Ford truck or a set of shiny new woodworking tools.

And Mama, well, Amalie just hoped she would understand.

With the pillowcase slung over her shoulder, she climbed out the window and slipped past the dog to make tracks for Papa's workshop. She found her suitcase easily enough and, before she could change her mind, put one foot in front of the other and passed down the long driveway to the main road.

From there she headed toward New Iberia, walking in the moonlit shadows of pines and cypress that had grown on these roads well before she was born.

Carrying a suitcase full of clothes and a pillowcase stuffed with her Bible and the quilt her mother made her for her fifteenth birthday made for slow going. Every few hundred yards Amalie had to stop and rest, and more than once she wished she hadn't left the cheese and bread to appease the dog upon its waking.

Then there was the heat. Though the day had long ended, the air felt thick and warm.

The night sky had begun to go pink on the horizon when Amalie heard the whine of tires on the road behind her. She wiped the perspiration from her forehead and turned to walk backward, unwilling to miss the approach of the vehicle lest Papa be chasing her.

The lights went from pinpricks to something akin to stage lights before a truck came into view. With grit she'd never realized she had, Amalie stuck out her thumb as the vehicle bounced by.

The truck groaned to a stop in the clearing ahead, revealing a load of melons tied beneath a net in the back. Amalie hurried to the passenger door and stood on tiptoe to peer inside. A white-haired man offered a stern look.

"What are you doing walking the roads this time of the morning?"

Amalie shrugged. "Trying to get to New Iberia."

Another stern look then a nod. "Get in then." He turned his attention to the road ahead. "Be quick about it."

Later, as she waited in line to spend half her egg money on a ticket to Hollywood, Amalie wondered if that man might race back to Latagnier to tell Papa where she'd gone. After all, most folks on the bayou knew one another.

If he recognized her, however, he never let on, and he

apparently didn't run back right away to the home place to tattle on her. This much was obvious when the bus rolled out of the station leaving New Iberia and her old life in a cloud of fumes.

five

Four days later, Amalie stared past the road grime on the window to behold the land of her dreams. Somewhere between Shreveport and Dallas she'd stopped trying to get comfortable and accepted the fact that sleep would be difficult as long as she rode the smoke-belching, bone-shattering, bouncing bus. By the time she reached Amarillo, she'd learned to sleep despite the inconvenience.

"Is that Paramount Studios?" she heard someone in the back of the bus ask.

"Sure is," another responded. "See, it says it right there."

Amalie gazed in awe at the ornate white concrete arch with its gold lettering. Sure enough, it was the famous studio. Behind those gates were real live movie stars. Closing her eyes, she tried to imagine what was going on in the many barnlike structures visible from the street.

Right this minute someone could be shooting a movie that people all over the world would watch. Why, the next *Gone With the Wind* or *Prisoner of Dreams* could be in production on the other side of the fence.

"*Mais, jamais de la vie.*" What a life.

"You some kind of foreigner?"

Amalie's eyes flew open to behold the blue-capped bus driver standing before her. In the place of the frown he'd worn for the past five hundred miles, he had put on a concerned look. "What? No."

He continued to stare. "You getting off or going with us to San Diego?"

"I'm sorry," she muttered as she gathered her pillowcase and stuffed her handbag inside. "Yes, I'm getting off here."

He shook his head. For the first time Amalie noticed he wore a patch on his shirt pocket embroidered with the name JOE. "Kids," he muttered as he removed his hat to scratch his bald head. "I'm sure your mama or daddy's about got tired of waiting by now."

Stunned, Amalie blinked away instant tears. When she'd recovered sufficiently to attempt a response, she realized he had returned to his seat to reach for a small notebook. By the time she'd collected her things and made the trudge from the middle of the bus, Joe had finished his scribbling and put the notebook away beside his seat.

"You need any help with your bags?" He leaned forward to look out the opened door. "I don't see anyone out there. You got someone coming to meet you?"

"Sort of," she said, averting her gaze as she rounded the corner and negotiated the steep stairs. She'd hoped the Lord would meet her there.

As her foot touched California soil, she exhaled sharply. Her journey was over.

Unfortunately, when she tried to put her other foot down on solid paving, she missed and stepped into a hole. A moment later her pillowcase went one way and her suitcase flew the other. She landed somewhere in between the two, with her bones—if not her pride—intact.

"Nice entrance," she whispered as she scrambled to her feet and swiped at the road dust decorating her best blue skirt.

"Actually I sort of liked it, except for the part where you stumbled," came a deep voice from somewhere behind her.

Amalie froze. As much as she wanted to give the smart aleck what for, she hated to face him. He solved the problem by reaching for her hand and turning her to face him.

A forward move, to be sure, and yet before she could scold the impertinent fellow, she caught a good look at him. Something she couldn't quite put her finger on stole the breath right out of her.

It wasn't his swarthy good looks, although to be sure his appearance was something to behold. No, the attraction, if she could call it that, ran much deeper. He also looked oddly familiar, as if she'd seen him before.

He thrust her suitcase toward her, and she took it and held it against her chest. "You dropped it," he said by way of explanation.

"Yes," she managed, "and I thank you."

There they stood, she the weary traveler çovered in the dust of at least five states and he the obviously polished-and-handsome man-about-town who looked as if he'd just stepped from a toothpaste ad. Never had Amalie felt so out of place as under the piercing gaze of this man.

And yet. . .

"Hey, Rob-o, you coming? Tillie's waiting."

Amalie looked past the man to see another man very much like him approaching. While that fellow was more movie-star handsome, this one, less perfect and more interesting, held her attention.

The man called *Rob-o* turned to offer a toothpaste-perfect smile to the approaching man. "Be right there, Ed." He shrugged as he returned his attention to Amalie. "You sure you're all right?"

She nodded.

His expression showed he didn't seem convinced, so she nodded again.

"Someone meeting you?" Rob looked past her then to the right and left. "I could wait with you until they get here."

Handsome *and* a gentleman. Amalie's heart did a flip-flop.

Then pride hit her hard. How could she let this man think she had no one to meet her and nowhere to go?

"No, really, thank you, but that's not necessary." She gathered up a smile and her things and strode past him with the hopes she could convey a confidence she did not feel.

ஃ

"Who was that?" Ed stood in the door of the Starlight Grill. "You didn't tell me you met all the pretty new Hollywood starlets at the bus station nowadays."

"Hush."

Rob gave his cousin a playful shove, causing enough distraction to give him a second to look back and see where the girl had wandered. He caught a glimpse of blue skirts and a cheap cardboard suitcase disappearing around the corner and had the strangest sensation he ought to go after her. He was about to do so when Ed caught him by the shoulder and dragged him on to the Starlight Grill.

"C'mon," Ed said in brusque Italian. "Signora Tillie is waiting."

The moment Rob crossed the threshold of the Starlight Grill he heard, "There's my fella."

Tillie's bear hug felt a little like wrestling with the real thing, especially today as she'd chosen to ignore the August heat in favor of a mink stole she claimed had been a gift from Rudolph Valentino. Rob stepped back to let the cloud of perfume-scented air pass then grinned.

"It's always good to see you, Miss Tillie," he said. "I see you're wearing the fur Mr. Valentino gave you. Is it the twenty-third already?"

She batted her lashes and puckered her lips into a frown. Tillie Rush might have given her heart to Jesus, but she did enjoy the occasional harmless flirtation.

"No, baby, it's just the ninth," she said gently, "but I was thinking about my Rudy last night and figured I'd go ahead and start early this year instead of waiting until the actual anniversary of his death. I'm not getting any younger, you know."

Rob held the tiny redhead at arm's length, narrowing his eyes. Not only did she sport Valentino's fur over her customary pink and white waitress uniform, but she also wore a silver charm bracelet she attributed to the elder Barrymore and a locket with her initials entwined with another pair rumored to belong to a member of the British royal family.

In all, Miss Tillie Rush had lived quite a life, at least until she found the Lord. Now her world seemed to revolve around the Starlight Grill and its interesting collection of employees, most of whom she had rescued in one way or another.

Even though he didn't work there, Rob counted himself among those Tillie called her darlings. "I don't believe for a moment that you're a day past thirty-nine, Tillie, dear. I think you've found the secret to eternal youth."

"Honey, the good Lord doesn't make that a secret. We all get the choice of taking Him up on His offer of eternal youth, just not in this life." Tillie toyed with the corner of her stole then peered up at Rob. "Me, I'm anxious to finish up with this one and get on with the next one. The Bible says we get new bodies, and I'm hoping He'll let me have my pick."

"Oh, Miss Tillie, there's nothing wrong with the one you've got," Ed said. "I still think you're the prettiest girl in the place."

Tillie swatted Ed on the arm and pointed toward the kitchen. "Get on now, Eduardo, darling," she said playfully. "Roberto and I have some business to discuss."

Roberto. Even his mother didn't call him by his given name.

"Come, let's have coffee," she said as she motioned to the corner booth near the front of the Starlight Grill. A few minutes later she'd poured two steaming mugs then doused hers liberally with milk and sugar.

Rob sipped at the strong black brew and waited. When Tillie set her mug down and leaned her elbows on the table, he smiled. "Why the serious look, Miss Tillie?"

"This is serious business," she said with no inflection of amusement. "Very serious."

"All right." Rob set his mug down and regarded his hostess. "Anything I can help with?"

She gave him a look then nodded. "In fact, there is."

"Anything," he said.

Tillie's blue eyes narrowed. "You better hear me out before you go and agree to something."

"Go ahead then," he said. "Tell me what I can do."

"Roberto, I've always been a plainspoken woman, even before the Lord got hold of me. I'm too old to change, so I'm just going to come right out with it." She paused. "I want you to take over the Starlight Grill."

Now that wasn't what he'd expected at all. A loan or perhaps advice on financial matters, maybe, but not this.

"Well, Miss Tillie, I, um. . ."

"See, I told you not to say yes until you heard the question." She reached for her mug then seemed to think better of it and put it down again. "Roberto, you are a levelheaded fellow and right easy on the eyes to boot."

"Thank you, Miss Tillie."

"And I know you got big dreams. You still flying those airplanes?"

"I am, when they're in working condition, that is."

She nodded. "I know you aim to make that your living someday. Your uncle, you and he still got that place down at the airpark?"

"Yes, ma'am. Uncle Gio and I are doing pretty well flying for the studios."

"But you don't want to do location work all your life, do you?"

Funny how this line of questioning felt so normal. "Actually I'd like someday to run a cargo fleet. Sort of like a big trucking company, only with planes. I think it's the wave of the future."

Tillie took it all in then smiled. "Yes, and I believe you'll be quite successful."

"Thank you," he said.

"But. . ." A troubled look crossed Tillie's ageless face.

Rob waited, fingers tapping the tabletop. "What?" he finally asked.

"This war," she said. "It's coming, and I don't think President Roosevelt can do anything about it."

Tillie's charm bracelet jingled, and Rob focused on the silver charms rather than their owner. "I suppose not," he said slowly.

Rob had his own feelings about the war. But for his father's strident objections and his mother's impassioned pleas, he would be in Europe flying for the Royal Air Force instead of sipping coffee with Tillie Rush. His parents had extracted a promise that he would remain a civilian unless war came to American shores. Sitting on the sidelines grated on him; but his father raised him to believe honor was more important than anything else, and unfortunately he'd given his word.

"You look confused, my son."

"I am." He reached for his mug and let a healthy swallow of Tillie's dark roast slide down his throat. "What does the war have to do with what you're asking of me?"

"Nothing at all, my darling," she said with a broad smile. "I'm just making small talk sound important until I can figure out how to tell you I need your help."

six

Amalie lay wide awake on the narrow cot in a hotel whose name she did not know, nor did she care. Its close proximity to the bus station and the low cost of a clean private room and bath were enough to cause her to part with a week's rent in advance. By next Saturday she hoped to have found other more permanent quarters.

This time the sound of a siren echoing as it passed on the street below didn't even make her blink. Instead she closed her eyes and waited until the room no longer pulsed brilliant red.

Sighing, Amalie turned away from the window and punched the thin pillow. She'd heard the same noise at least a half dozen times since she checked in this afternoon. Such was the surprise at hearing something so loud moving so fast that the first time or two she'd flown to the open window and stuck her head out to watch a patrol car as it disappeared around the corner.

There were few reasons other than New Year's Eve and Fourth of July celebrations to blare such a warning on the bayou.

The bayou.

Amalie fisted the threadbare sheet and dabbed her eyes. "I will not cry," she said softly. "I am not a child, and I refuse to act like one. Besides, the Lord wants me here. You do, don't You, heavenly Father?"

Silence.

Amalie ducked her head and cried in earnest. Finally spent, she sniffed hard then closed her eyes.

When sleep would not come, she rose to walk the fifteen

43

steps between the door and the window. She began a dozen letters to Mama, her sisters, Ernest, and even one to Papa. None of them got past the first few words.

What would she say? "I'm gone." They knew that. The reason she left? Well, that was obvious to anyone who'd known Amalie for more than a few weeks.

Nothing seemed right, so she wadded each letter and tossed them into the bent trash can under the bathroom sink. A postcard to say she arrived safely would be the best she could do at the moment. Tomorrow she would purchase one and address it to the entire family.

That should suffice for now. Besides, postage costs would be much less. With half her savings spent on the bus ticket and a good portion of the rest spent on the room where she now paced, Amalie knew she would have to find a job soon.

First thing tomorrow she would march up to the gates at Paramount Studios. Of course she knew the odds were that she wouldn't start with on-screen employment, but she was willing to take lesser work to get her foot in the door.

The thought of walking where movie stars had tread kept her mind racing even as her body begged for sleep. She tore a page from the tablet she used as a journal and began another letter to Mama and Papa. Three times she tried, and three times she failed. Words, her former friends, were nowhere to be found, at least not the right ones. Finally she moved the pillow to the end of the bed and reached for the pillowcase she'd used as a second suitcase.

Beyond caring about the road grime the case wore, she slipped it over the thin hotel pillow then tucked her quilt around her. The faint scent of Mama's old woodstove combined with that of cotton air-dried in the Louisiana sun teased her nostrils and lulled her to sleep.

ঌ

She turned on her side and snuggled deep within the cocoon

of the quilt until the orange glow faded to black, vaguely aware that she had not spent the night in her own bed. As the reality of her situation dawned, she closed her eyes tighter and tried to pray. Rather than the cozy dialogue she generally held with the Lord, all she could say was, "Heavenly Father, what have I done?"

How long Amalie held her eyes shut and her heart open to God, she had no idea. Somewhere between trying to pray and giving up, her bladder and stomach began to complain. Finally she rose and let the bath and the stale toast saved from yesterday morning's breakfast at the truck stop take care of her immediate needs.

After she washed her face and hands and ran a comb through her hair, she felt a little better. The homesickness still threatened, but anticipation of the adventure that lay before her held it temporarily at bay. She would have to make today a good day, or tonight would be more of the same: sirens and self-pity.

Maybe the Lord would speak louder out in His creation— what a body could find of it among the tall buildings and sparse green areas of this part of the city. Still, it didn't hurt to look.

Besides, she might even see a movie star or two.

Folding the quilt back into the pillowcase, Amalie set them aside then made her bed. She took one quick look in the mirror, snagged her handbag, and headed downstairs to look for work, movie stars, and possibly her big break. She got all the way to the gates of the Paramount Studios before she realized today was Sunday.

Oh, no. Amalie's heart sank as she leaned against the wall separating her from the movie studio.

Just a week ago she'd been sitting in the church pew back in Latagnier thinking about California. How ironic to be standing in front of Paramount Studios seven days later thinking about Latagnier.

But this was the first Sunday she'd missed church since she was a little girl and sick with the fever. She'd been in the hospital then. This time she had no excuse beyond the fact that she'd been so consumed with leaving home that she'd forgotten how many days had passed.

Amalie paused in front of a newsstand intending to look at the postcards. After choosing a red one spelling out Hollywood in letters containing photographs of landmarks around town, she turned her attention to the variety of newspaper and magazines on display. One in particular, listing casting calls and studio updates, caught her attention, and she reached to purchase it along with the postcard. A car horn honked, and she jumped, nearly dropping her handbag.

"Jittery little thing, aren't you?" The proprietor placed three quarters and a dime on the counter then looked up. "You'd think you weren't from around here," he said with a leer.

Ignoring the man, Amalie slipped the coins into her purse and took a step away.

"Hey! Maybe you'd like someone to show you around. An older fellow with some class." He glanced down at her reading material then back at her. "Yeah, that's right. Class and an in at the studios. Which one you wanna work for, girlie?"

Cradling the paper and postcard against her chest, she left the newsstand and the awful man behind. She crossed the street, weaving around cars stopped at the light, and turned the corner to race a full block before she slowed her pace.

Papa's words of warning against the world outside the bayou echoed, but she pushed them away. As much as she loved her father, the man had no idea what it was like to be a modern woman seeking out a modern career.

Amalie shifted her handbag to the other arm and reached for her handkerchief. Blotting at her forehead, she sighed. August in Louisiana was nearly unbearable, but she never expected the heat to follow her all the way to the Pacific Ocean.

Up ahead, a six-foot-tall neon ice cream cone beckoned, affixed to the roof of a diner. As she walked beneath the cone, she saw a hand-lettered notice next to the CLOSED sign.

"Waitress wanted," she read.

—*Well, now. Maybe, just until I can get a real job*—

"What am I thinking?" Amalie straightened her spine and picked up her pace. "I didn't come to Hollywood to work in a diner. The Lord called me to be a star, not a waitress."

But as she walked away, doubt slithered up her spine. The Lord brought her to this place, of that she felt certain. The part about being a star, well, was that her desire or God's?

"I'll give it a month."

≈

Tuesday, September 16

Rob left three half-pound patties sizzling on the grill to step into the alley and mop his forehead. He'd never been afraid of manual labor, but nothing he'd taken on in the past had ever been as demanding as the job he'd agreed to do for Tillie.

Of course, she'd asked him to run the place, not work the grill, but it hadn't taken any time for Rob to realize his cousin Ed made a much better manager than he. And neither of them could wait tables well at all.

"I hope you're happy, Miss Tillie," he said as he looked to the sky. "I never imagined you'd leave us."

In truth, the only thing more surprising than Tillie Rush's abrupt departure from Hollywood for parts unknown was his agreeing to take over the Starlight Grill—on a strictly temporary basis, of course. Tillie promised she would return soon.

"She'd better," he muttered. "And, Lord, if You're listening, would You send me a couple of waitresses to help? I had no idea how hard it was to run a diner."

The familiar hum of an aircraft caught his attention, and

he shielded his hand against the glare to watch it approach overhead. A California Clipper, he decided—the pride of the Pan Am fleet and an aircraft he dreamed of sitting behind the controls of once again.

The last time he'd flown a Boeing 314 like the one now soaring overhead was back in '39. Freshly graduated from South Carolina's Citadel, he'd been about to accept a job as a crewmember on the Yankee Clipper flying their new transatlantic mail route when news of the war in Europe arrived at Casa Tratelli. He turned Pan Am down, deciding to head for England to join the Royal Air Force.

But rather than fighting the war in Europe, Rob had given in to his parents' pleas and ended up working on aircraft engines and flying for the studios with Uncle Gio and flipping burgers for Tillie in Hollywood.

Of course, Rob had known all along that flying copilot on the Clipper was only a stepping-stone to his real dream. Someday aviation technology would allow businesses to fly their goods around the world economically, and with the Lord's help he intended to be in on the ground floor. The first of what he hoped to be a large fleet sat waiting for him in pieces in a hangar at the Adams Port Airport in North Hollywood.

And then there was the ever-present possibility that the United States might join the war, providing Rob with another career, that of army pilot. He'd relish that, should the need arise, but he certainly had no wish for war to come to this country.

Still, it looked more every day like that would happen. Just last week, President Roosevelt had issued a shoot-on-sight order against all German and Italian vessels. It was only a matter of time before things escalated to the point where the president was declaring actual war.

War was such an ugly thing, and yet he'd go to his grave

defending the freedom he had here. He'd heard too many stories from his Italian relatives to take his citizenship and his rights lightly.

Rob sighed. There would be time to dream of planes and worry about war. Right now hungry diners were awaiting his culinary expertise. Rob chuckled with that thought as he returned to the kitchen. Expertise was an overstatement at best. Anything beyond burgers and scrambled eggs were better left to Ed.

Speaking of Ed, where was he? A quick glance out the pass-through into the dining room revealed his cousin was not in his usual spot behind the counter.

"Probably sitting with a pretty girl again."

For all his good points Ed was a notorious ladies' man. Rob suspected his cousin had taken up employment with Tillie as much for the interaction with the current and future starlets visiting the nearby Paramount Studios as for the steady work and decent pay.

Rob made short work of finishing the three burgers then hit the bell and waited for his cousin to appear. When no answer came, Rob loaded the plates onto a tray and headed into the dining room to place them in front of a trio of elderly men seated at the counter.

In the far corner he found Ed seated in a booth, his back to the kitchen. Across from him sat a lovely dark-haired woman. Irritation flared. While he was sweating over a hot grill in the kitchen, his cousin, the ladies' man, was taking it easy with another future Mignon Dupree.

Great. I'll put an end to that right now.

He tossed his apron on the back of the nearest stool and headed in their direction. In quick Italian Rob said, "Eduardo, you'd better be interviewing a waitress because otherwise I'm going to—"

Words froze in his throat, and his mind went blank. Surely

he'd seen beautiful brown-eyed girls before. They were a dime a dozen, especially in Hollywood. But this one. . .

Their gazes met. Again he tried and failed to find his voice.

Rob had the vaguest impression of Ed rising, of something being said about a new waitress and then a name. Amalie. He nodded toward her and muttered a word of greeting.

As far as he knew he'd never been in love, but something deep inside him told him this must be what it felt like. Odd, and yet it didn't seem so.

"And this is my cousin," Ed said.

"Rob," he managed.

"Pleased to meet you, Rob," she said in a voice dripping with moonlight and magnolias.

Like his mother, this one was a daughter of the South if he'd ever heard one. And in a moment of clarity, Rob realized he was a goner.

He grasped her hand in his, acutely aware of the childlike size of her fingers and the coolness of her palm. And yet when she rose, he could see she was a tall woman, nearly his height, and slender as a reed. As Rob released his grip, her hand slid across his palm, and with a start he felt the calluses.

She quickly turned her attention to Ed. "You do understand this is just temporary, Mr. Cantoni."

Ed nodded. "Yeah, I understand, doll." He looked at Rob. "Miss Breaux's only going to be with us a short while." He winked. "Until she gets discovered."

"Discovered?"

"Why, yes," she said slowly. "I'm not a waitress, you see. I'm an—"

"Actress?" Rob interjected.

Again their gazes met, and this time her brown eyes were open wide to reveal threads of gold woven against dark centers. She blinked, and her long lashes dusted cheeks freshly colored bright pink. Her shaking fingers tucked an ebony curl behind her dainty ear as she ducked her head.

"Yes," she said. "I believe I've been called to be an actress. I intend to find work soon."

Without a word, Rob turned and walked away.

seven

Amalie had been employed nearly a week at the Starlight Grill, and the cook hadn't said a word to her beyond what was required. Oh, he'd been friendly enough, and he'd certainly been a gentleman when it came to opening doors and such, but a strange wall of ice stood between them that all the Southern charm she possessed couldn't break through.

If he were any other unfriendly fellow she might have given up by now, but there was something about him. Something different.

Something interesting.

Ed Cantoni had more than made up for his cousin's less than charming personality. After a few days of asking for dates, he'd realized Amalie intended only a friendship between them. The diner's manager had taken the situation in stride and responded with gentlemanly good humor.

Watching Rob out of the corner of her eye, Amalie pretended to scrub a spot off the counter. He seemed oblivious to her, busy working numbers on a tablet, although more than once she'd caught him looking her way. Finally she decided enough was enough.

Amalie tossed the dishcloth beneath the counter and strolled toward the kitchen. "Two slices of apple pie, please," she said casually.

He looked up from his duties and frowned then looked past her to the empty dining room. "I didn't hear anyone come in."

Gazing at him, she shrugged. "They didn't."

"Oh."

He didn't move so she did, reaching past him to retrieve a pair of plates and forks off the drain board. She cut two generous slices of pie and set one atop his table.

"Hey, do you mind? I was doing something here."

"I see that," she said as she scooted the nearest stool up to the counter beside him.

The cook tried to glare but wasn't successful. Instead his gaze swept over her face and landed on the pie.

Amalie waited a second to see if he would have anything further to say. When he didn't, she dove into her pie with gusto. It wasn't nearly as good as Mama's, but it wasn't bad.

"You don't eat like any *movie star* I've ever met."

His first words in nearly a week. Of course, given his inexplicable irritation at her presence, they *would* have to be sarcastic ones.

Fine. Two could play at that game.

"Oh, really?" She stabbed an apple slice and downed it. "You see a lot of movie stars, do you?"

The cook's shoulders straightened, and he stared at her as if she'd just asked him something awful. "What if I do?" he asked gruffly.

Well, now, that hadn't turned out as she expected. Amalie searched about for a response that might make the cranky cook smile.

"I suppose I'd have to wonder where else you worked because you certainly don't see them in here." She punctuated the statement with another mouthful of apple pie, this time heavy on the crust.

His gaze met hers. She braced herself for the next cutting comment. Instead he grinned.

Rob Cantoni, grouch extraordinaire, actually smiled.

Oh, but he was handsome when he smiled. His eyes, usually a steel gray like winter in Louisiana, sparkled like

Mama's polished silver, and he had the most adorable laugh lines at each corner.

The man she thought of as old suddenly looked to be near her own age.

How very interesting.

"You just don't work the right shift, Miss Breaux," he said as he tasted a mouthful of pie.

"I suppose not, Mr. Cantoni," she replied.

Funny, but he flinched when she said his name. He must not like being addressed in such a proper manner. Probably comes with spending his life as a fry cook.

Well, I don't care. He could be lord of a fine manor, and it wouldn't matter to me. I find this fellow very interesting.

He took another bite then pushed away the plate and picked up his pencil. A moment later he'd returned to his ciphering as if she weren't seated two feet away.

Amalie finished her pie then washed her plate and fork and set it on the drain to dry. She reached for his, and he placed his hand over hers. She drew back, jolted by the feelings the simple contact caused.

"I'm not finished," he said, meeting her stare with hooded eyes.

"All right then." She wiped her hands and straightened her apron. With the cook still watching, Amalie made a hasty exit. A few minutes later she walked past the kitchen to see him still staring at the door she'd disappeared through.

Oh, yes. This one is very interesting indeed.

❧

The supper crowd had come and gone, and Rob was exhausted. He secured the back door and tossed his apron into the linen hamper.

Of all the nights for Ed to be off, it had to be this one. Every bone in his body ached, and he knew when he pulled off his shoes tonight he'd find a bruise on the top of his foot where a can of tomato sauce had landed. He had a nasty burn on his left hand and a scrape on his elbow where he tripped taking the garbage out to the alley.

To top it off, he'd spent a good part of last evening—his only night away from the diner—with Uncle Gio down at the airpark. They'd alternated between working on the plane and listening to radio reports on the capture of Kiev by the Germans. Following the news a program broadcasted a spirited discussion between two politicians of why uncaring Americans were sitting home on their duffs and allowing Europe to be plundered. Finally Uncle Gio had turned off the old Philco radio and changed the subject to the Anaheim Aces' pitching woes, but the damage had been done.

Rob was one of those Americans sitting at home on his duff, and he knew it. Of course it wasn't that he didn't care— he did. If only he hadn't made a promise to Pop.

The memory put him in a bad mood all over again. Then he thought about the pie. An apple-pie peace offering served by the prettiest girl in Hollywood.

A girl who wanted to be a star.

Quick as that, Rob's bad mood returned. He snapped off the kitchen lights and snagged the front door keys.

On nights like tonight he almost wished he hadn't been so stubborn about making it on his own. A ride back to Brentwood in the back of Pop's Rolls and a spell in the sauna followed by a hot bath sounded wonderful about now. Instead he and his pride would take the short walk back to his apartment on Londonderry View.

Not pride, he corrected, but reliance on God put him where he was. As his gaze swept the diner, he had to admit that while his finances might never match his father's, his walk with the Lord had grown stronger each day.

"And that is a blessing no man can put a price on."

"Did you say something?"

Rob jumped, his attention directed to the slender brunette standing a few feet away. "I thought you'd left."

The girl shook her head. "I wanted to finish this first." She tucked what looked like a postcard into her handbag then placed the pencil in the drawer beneath the counter. "I can do it later."

"I'm not in a hurry," he said.

Her worried face softened. "Are you sure?"

He wasn't, and yet he said the opposite. What was wrong with him?

"I won't be but a minute."

She retrieved the pencil and held the tip inches from the postcard. Twice she touched the tip to the paper but both times stopped short of actually writing anything. Finally she printed something in the address column.

Progress at last.

Rob watched a moment then pretended to busy himself folding newspapers and setting them in place beside the register. Next he filled the salt and pepper shakers, a job generally reserved for the morning shift.

A couple of times he heard what sounded like the scratching of pencil on paper, but closer attention revealed the woman to be erasing rather than writing. Salt and pepper shakers full, he graduated to catsup containers and finally to rolling napkins. The clock above the kitchen door ticked onward, and with each staccato beat Rob's irritation rose.

Why had he agreed to wait in the first place? It was almost as if—no, he refused to consider the possibility that the Lord might want him stuck here with Amalie Breaux. That would be too much of a stretch, even for his fertile imagination.

He cast another glance at his companion, who now scribbled rather than erased. What would the Lord want of him in relation to this Louisiana girl?

"All done," she said. "*Merci beaucoup, monsieur.*"

Rob looked up sharply. "You speak French?"

"Oh, did I say that in French? I'm sorry. I guess my mind was back home."

His heart wrenched as he watched her expression go wistful. He'd seen it a hundred times, and yet homesickness never looked so beautiful on a girl as it did on Amalie Breaux.

Steeling his heart, Rob shook his head. "You know, I guess I'll never understand why people come out here thinking it's some kind of place where their dreams will come true. Most of them sit around moping and wishing they were back home, but their pride won't let them admit they ought to give up and go home. It's a pity most folks don't get the fact that the movies are *not* real life and movie people aren't any less confused and unhappy than the average Joe. More, generally."

Her wide eyes looked ready to tear up. Her lower lip quivered as her fingers worried with the postcard.

Rob held up his hands. "Look—I'm sorry, honey. I didn't mean to upset you. It was just an observation."

eight

Just an observation. Amalie blinked back the tears and sucked in a deep breath. By the time she let it out, she'd gained some measure of control.

"It sounds as if you've been in Hollywood a long time, Mr. Cantoni."

Again he cringed. Was it the question or the formal use of his name that caused the cook discomfort?

"Just call me Rob, would you? Cantoni's not my. . .that is, I'm really. . ."

He seemed to have run out of words. An awkward moment passed while Amalie waited.

Well, now. What to do?

"All right, Rob." She left the pencil on the counter and gathered up her handbag. "Thank you for staying to keep me company so I could finish the postcard." She paused. "I apologize for taking so long. It was a bit. . .difficult to write."

To his credit, the cook asked no further questions nor made any more observations. Rather he walked her to the door then locked up and escorted her as far as the corner.

"You live far?" he asked, his fists jammed into his pockets and his attention focused at a point somewhere past her.

"No," she said carefully. "Not far at all."

"All right then." He rocked back on his heels. "I'll be heading home."

As he seemed in no hurry, Amalie felt it only polite to ask, "Do you live far?"

"Nah." He turned his attention to her. Still he did not move. "Are you going to be all right? Walking home the rest of the way by yourself, I mean."

58

Surely he didn't mistake her for some cowering ninny. For all the world the man sounded like Papa. Always thinking some awful danger was lurking about and set to cause harm.

"I'll be fine," she said brusquely.

"I see," was his terse response.

"I'm going that way." She pointed in the direction of the bus station and the hotel. "Good night then."

Rob muttered a quick response then headed in the opposite direction. Amalie fumbled with her key then turned to walk toward the place she'd come to think of as home.

Her companion's footsteps echoed a few more beats then faded as he turned the corner. "I don't know what to make of you, Rob Cantoni." She paused to chuckle. "*Just* Rob, that is," she said, imitating his gruff voice.

Amalie crossed the empty street as the night breeze blew past, lifting the ends of her hair and reminding her of home. How often had she and the others escaped to the relative coolness of the sleeping porch with pillow and blanket?

Or, in Amalie's case, with the quilt that now waited for her up in the room.

Glancing up at the starlit night, she thought of the evenings spent counting constellations and wishing on falling stars. Another pang of homesickness hit, and she squared her shoulders, refusing to give in.

"That was then, and this is now," she whispered. "I will see stars other than the ones up there in the sky. And if the Lord allows, one day I will be one of them."

She paused at the mailbox and drew the postcard from her handbag. "*Je t'aime, Mama, et Papa,*" she whispered as she lightly kissed the postcard then slipped it into the box.

A second later she hit the ground with a sickening thud. Pain danced across her head, down her back, and returned to lodge between her eyes.

Amalie blinked hard and tried to focus. What happened?

Then she realized that somehow, between her and the stars glittering in the Hollywood sky, stood a man.

A man with a knife.

🙠

Rob chided himself for worrying about a woman who could obviously take care of herself, and yet he remained out of sight but nearby. A few more minutes and he'd peek out to be sure the girl got home safely.

After all, this was hardly the best part of Hollywood, even during the day. Unless she lied about where she lived, the only place a woman could live in this neighborhood was the hotel across from the bus station.

Not exactly the Hollywood Roosevelt.

In fact, the place looked seedy at best, and not a spot where he would leave any of his female relatives for five minutes, much less overnight.

Or, in Miss Breaux's case, obviously longer than that.

Rob stared up at the night sky and found Orion's Belt then the Big Dipper. He searched for the Little Dipper and traced its collection of stars across the sky. Funny, he hadn't taken the time to enjoy the stars in far too long. But then he'd preferred to fly among them rather than peer up at them from the ground.

A woman's scream pierced the night.

Bolting from his hiding place, Rob made short work of retracing his steps. He arrived at the corner where they'd parted in time to see a shadow moving on the other side of the mailbox about halfway down the block.

He moved carefully, keeping to the dark side of the walkway. Until he saw the glint of something shiny.

A knife in one hand—and a handbag in the other.

Rob picked up his pace, treading lightly across the intersection. A few yards from where the man stood, he broke into a run. Tackling the creep with a running leap, he rolled with him into the gutter, jerked the waitress's purse from his grasp, and tossed it in her direction.

Something sharp jabbed against his rib, and he reached for the man's arm. A scuffle ensued, ending when Rob managed to kick the wind out of the guy's lungs and the weapon out of his hand at the same time.

Thoughts of giving chase when the fellow fled disappeared when he looked over at the waitress. Amalie Breaux leaned against the mailbox cradling her handbag, shocked but seemingly none the worse for wear.

"Did he hurt you?" Rob demanded.

"No."

Not trusting her to judge, he gave her a quick look over. "You've got a nasty bump on the back of your head. Did you fall, or did he hit you?"

"I. . .don't know. I think he might have hit me."

He helped her to her feet and walked her to the hotel's dimly lit front entrance. A glance inside revealed a bellhop fast asleep on a luggage cart and two men playing cards at the check-in counter. A fluorescent light gave the room an eerie green cast, while the stained and ripped furniture looked as if it had been dragged in from the curb on trash day.

Rob led the still-stunned woman by the elbow, taking her from the entrance to the elevator. "What floor?" Amalie blinked several times but said nothing. A thought occurred to him, and he acted on it.

"Sur quel plancher est-il votre pièce, Amalie?"

She seemed surprised, but she cleared her throat to respond. *"Deux."*

"All right then. Let's go." He pushed the button for the second floor then wrapped his arm around Amalie's waist to keep her upright. When the doors opened, Rob helped her off.

"Quatorze," she said without being asked, and together they trudged toward room number fourteen.

Amalie produced the key but fumbled in trying to fit it into the lock. Rob took over and got her inside in short order. Despite its starkness the room held a measure of charm, due in part to the mix of flowers in the drinking glass on the nightstand and the multicolored quilt folded neatly over the end of the bed. Only the stack of *Daily Variety* and assorted screen magazines decorating the dressing table gave him pause.

Until this moment he'd forgotten she aspired to a movie career.

"*Merci*," Amalie mumbled as she sank onto the straight-back chair nearest the door.

Rob shook off his feelings about the woman's career choice and strode across the room to switch on the hotplate. "You're welcome."

"*Je serai beau maintenant.*"

He grabbed the teapot and filled it in the bathroom sink then placed it sizzling on the red ring of the hotplate. "I beg to differ. You're not fine now at all. Do you have any coffee?"

When she shook her head, he asked about teabags. She pointed to a shelf where a stack of teabags wedged into a cracked green mug sat beside a tin of cookies and a box of noodle soup mix. A matching mug, a jelly-jar drinking glass, and a slightly bent spoon rounded out her meager kitchen supplies.

Fifteen minutes later he'd coaxed Amalie into finishing her tea. Much of her color had returned, and the tremor had disappeared from her hand. "*Voulez-vous un petit gateau?*" he asked.

"No cookies for me, thanks." She set the mug on the table and rose.

Rob stood as well.

"It's well past midnight, and I shouldn't keep you any longer. Thank you, Mr.—" She cleared her throat. "I mean, thank you, *Rob.*"

"Think nothing of it," he said with a roll of his shoulders. Someday he'd have to set her straight on his last name, but not tonight. "Rescuing damsels in distress is a sideline of mine." When she said nothing, he pointed to the door. "I'll be going then," he said. "That is, if you feel like you can sleep."

"Of course. As I said, I'll be fine."

The tremble in her voice and the way she seemed to look through him rather than at him gave her away. The color flooding her cheeks moments ago had faded. She would be fine eventually, but not tonight.

Tonight she would need to know someone was looking out for her.

"*S'endormir maintenant. Vous êtes sûr.*" When she gave him a blank look, he repeated in English, "Go to sleep now. You're safe." He added, "I'll be here. And I won't let anyone bother you."

"*Oui.*"

Unsure whether she gave him a nod of agreement or dismissal, he glanced over his shoulder as he stepped into the hall. Propriety would never allow him to remain inside the room.

He'd have to figure out another way.

nine

"Papa?"

Amalie awoke with a start and sat bolt upright, clutching the quilt to her chest. Reality hit her in stages; like waves washing on the beach, the thoughts pushed then pulled at her until she became aware of her surroundings.

She'd dreamed of home again. This time about the night the children told ghost stories on the sleeping porch until Papa had to be called to sleep among them.

Little did they know Papa's snoring would keep them awake far longer than any scary tale.

There it was again. What was that racket? Why, it almost sounded like. . .

It sounded like Papa. She shook her head.

Like snoring.

Wrapping the quilt around her shoulders, she edged toward the source of the sound: the hall outside her door. In light of last night's events, opening the door took a large measure of courage, but she managed.

"I'm fine, and I can't be a 'fraidy-cat forever," she whispered. "I've got to—"

Snort. Groan. Whistle.

Amalie jumped back from the partially opened door, tripping over the quilt. She hit the threadbare carpet with a thud, surely adding a bruise to her posterior to match the one on the back of her head.

A sheepish Rob leaned inside, his hair spiked on one side

and flattened on the other where he'd obviously slept on it. His once perfectly pressed shirt had wrinkled, and one side of his collar stuck straight up.

"I'm sorry. Did I wake you?" he asked, his voice thick with sleep.

Recovering, Amalie scrambled to cover her buttoned-to-the-neck granny gown with the quilt. "Did you sleep out there?"

He scratched at the stubble on his chin. "Do you always answer a question with a question?"

"Do *you*?"

An impasse reached, each stared at the other, neither willing to look away. Amalie saw the humor of the situation, and the poor fellow's current bedraggled condition tugged at her heart. If ever she'd seen a knight in shining armor, Rob-the-Starlight-Grill-cook was definitely one.

Well, maybe a knight in slightly rumpled armor.

She laughed first, but Rob laughed louder. So loud, in fact, that a man down the hall opened his door to complain.

Funny how no one had minded the snoring.

"I should be going." Rob gripped the door frame then stood and swiped at his unruly hair. "Didn't help, did it?"

Amalie looked up at the mess he'd made of his hair. Even in this state, the man looked adorable. "The truth?"

"There you go answering a question with a question again." He shrugged. "Leave me one last shred of my dignity and ignore the one about my hair, would you?"

Amalie reached out to rest her hand on his arm. "Rob," she said slowly, "thank you."

He looked distinctly uncomfortable. Of course, a man who'd slept propped against a door deserved to feel out of sorts.

"As I said last night"—he raked at his hair again then looked down at her, the expression on his face now looking more bewildered than bothered—"rescuing damsels in distress is a particular specialty of mine, but you're welcome all the same."

"Stop teasing. I'm serious."

Rob laced his fingers with hers and lifted her hand to touch his lips. She looked away. A girl on her way up in Hollywood couldn't risk love with a fry cook.

It went against everything she believed to end the quest for what she believed God wanted for her. Not until the Lord said so, anyway.

He must have sensed her reluctance, for a moment later Rob released his grip. "Yes, well," he said as he looked away, "I'll see you at work this afternoon."

"Actually Ed told me I could have today off." She smiled despite the awkward situation. "I have an audition."

"An audition." Rob said the words as if she'd told him she was trying out for the position of dog catcher.

Amalie refused to let his bad humor temper her excitement. She offered a smile. "So I'll see you tomorrow at the diner."

"Tomorrow," he said with a shrug. "Sure."

With that, he was gone.

Amalie leaned out to watch Rob stride down the hall and stab the elevator button, all the while trying to tuck his shirttail back into his trousers. A moment later he disappeared inside the double doors.

Oh, yes, he is one interesting fellow. If only I knew the Lord had sent me here for something other than to serve Him in the movies.

She shut the door and strolled to the window in time to see Rob emerge onto the street. At the mailbox he paused then briskly set off walking again.

When she could no longer see him, Amalie gathered her thoughts and centered them on the afternoon ahead. Her first movie audition was no small matter, but she only felt the tiniest niggle of concern. Why should she be afraid? The Lord was with her, and through Him she could do anything.

❧

After the audition, however, she had a whole new perspective on what the Lord would allow. In this case, He had undoubtedly allowed her to fail miserably.

Oh, things started out fine. She'd been ushered through the majestic gates of Imperial Studios at precisely three o'clock, past oversize barnlike buildings with numbers painted on their sides and into a narrow, windowless room with three dozen women who looked remarkably like her.

By four she'd ceased praying and started counting ceiling tiles. By five it was over.

She'd been sent home the same way she came in, never having met a director, a producer, or anyone else remotely connected with making a movie. Her closest connection to anything related to motion pictures was to be warned out of the path of Clark Gable's limousine by the security guard at the gate.

The limo was empty, but surely Mr. Gable had recently sat inside it. Where she came from, that counted for something.

She decided to mention the encounter to Mama in her next letter. Wouldn't Mama be thrilled to hear she'd finally come close to a movie star?

Amalie paused and waited for the light to turn. No, she decided, Mama wouldn't be the least bit impressed.

The only thing Mama wanted to see written in a letter from Amalie was the arrival time of the bus bringing her home. And since Amalie had no plans—or money—to return to Louisiana, leastwise not anytime soon, Mama would have to settle for a report of Mr. Gable's shiny black limousine.

With the dinner hour just getting started, Amalie decided to head for the diner rather than go directly back to her empty hotel room. It was Thursday night, meatloaf night, and the place would be packed. Without a waitress, Ed and Rob would be in a panic by now.

Amalie opened the door to see the cousins juggling trays, neither with much success. Ed saw her first, and his smile warmed her heart. She might not be wanted at Imperial Studios, but tonight she was definitely needed at the Starlight Grill.

Then she caught sight of Rob. He stood in silhouette, head and shoulders visible as he leaned over the stove.

"Mashing potatoes?" she asked as she slipped past Rob to don her apron. He looked up, and she met his gaze and returned his smile. Funny, his grin didn't quite match the intensity of Ed's.

"Something like that," he muttered. "Didn't expect to see you here tonight. Thought you were busy putting Vivien Leigh out of a job." He slammed the pot lid atop the potatoes then stepped past her to disappear into the storeroom.

ten

The last diner left a few minutes after nine, and Ed quickly followed to turn the sign on the door to read "CLOSED." While Ed cleared the last table and hauled the dishes into the kitchen, Amalie scrubbed at a tomato sauce stain, certain the counter would never come clean.

"Here, let me apply some elbow grease."

Amalie looked up to see Ed standing next to her. He caught the dishrag she tossed then went to work on the counter.

"So how'd the audition go?" he asked.

Reaching for the basket of clean napkins, she picked up one and began to fold it. "Oh, I guess you could say it wasn't what I expected."

"Oh?" Ed looked up from his work. "What does that mean?"

Sighing, she reached for another napkin. "Well, I—"

"Amalie," Rob called from the kitchen, "you have a minute?"

She met Ed's amused gaze. "Would you excuse me?"

He nodded. "To be continued."

"Right," she said as she rounded the corner and entered the kitchen. To her surprise Rob stood at the back door staring up at the night sky. "Did you want to see me?"

Rather than turn to face her, he motioned for her to join him. When she did, she stopped short. The sky was ablaze with tiny pinpoints of light.

It reminded her of home.

"See that up there? It's Orion's Belt."

"Yes, I see it." She'd spent endless hours on the porch with Papa learning the constellations and watching for falling stars. "I'm surprised at how many stars you can see in the city."

69

Rob's soft sigh was barely audible. "You should see what they look like out in the canyon. Takes your breath away and reminds you of God's awesomeness all at the same time."

"I would like that very much."

He looked down at her, and his mood toward her softened. "Would you?"

Words failed her, so she settled for a nod.

"I think," he said as he leaned in her direction, "that it would be difficult to look at the stars when you're around."

Amalie felt herself drawn into his gaze, a magnet being pulled toward solid iron. She forced herself to blink before staring into Rob's eyes. "You speak French."

"*Oui.*"

"He also speaks Italian, Spanish, and passable German." Amalie jerked her attention toward Ed, who now sat at the kitchen counter folding napkins. "Yes, indeed. My cousin Rob would make a good secret agent, what with all the languages he knows and the secrets he keeps. Isn't that right, Mr. *Cantoni?*"

Suddenly the cook was all business. He ushered Amalie inside then closed and locked the back door. Barely sparing his cousin a passing glance, Rob stormed out of the kitchen and beat a path across the dining room to the door. Amalie retraced her steps into the dining room to take her handbag from beneath the counter.

Ed shrugged and offered a smile. "Looks like you're ready to leave. We can talk about that audition of yours another time."

Amalie shrugged. "I'll save you the trouble. Nothing happened."

Ed set the last folded napkin on top of the pile. "Nothing?"

She shook her head. "I sat in a chair for hours on end. Finally they told us we could go, so I did."

"That's odd." Ed scratched his chin. "Usually they at least ask you to read lines or walk. Didn't they call your name?"

"But how would they know my name?"

Ed looked at her, his brows raised. "Didn't you sign in?"

"Sign in?"

Her heart sank. No wonder she'd never been called into the audition room. *I'm such a knucklehead.*

Before she could respond, Rob returned to press his hand against the small of her back and lead her to the front door. "Lock it up, Ed," he called as the bells on the door jingled. "I'm walking Miss Breaux home. It's not safe for a lady to be out at this time of night."

"I could do that," Ed said, smiling.

"Good night, Ed," Rob said firmly as he ushered Amalie outside.

At the curb Rob slowed his pace to fall into step with her. A chill wind stole past, and she gave thanks that she'd included a warm sweater in her suitcase. Hollywood might stay temperate during the day, but once the sun went down the weather cooled off quickly.

"It's nice out tonight," she said with as much cheer as she could muster. She was too focused on what she'd done wrong this afternoon to think about the present.

If only she'd known to sign in at the audition. *I doubt Mignon Dupree and Clark Gable ever sat through a casting call without signing in.*

They walked in silence for a few more minutes. Amalie decided that conversation with Rob had to be less upsetting than the dialogue going on in her head, so she tried again.

"Are you from around here?"

He gave her a sideways glance. "Around here?"

"California." His blank stare caused her to try to be more specific. "Los Angeles? Hollywood, maybe?"

"Neither," he responded.

"Oh."

A couple of rebuffed attempts at conversation and Amalie

quit trying. If the cook wanted silence, then silence he would have. Besides, he'd already established that his home was somewhere west of here while hers was east.

At the intersection they would part ways. A shiver teased her spine, and it had nothing to do with the temperature.

"What are you doing?" she asked when he crossed the street along with her. "You live that way."

Still he said nothing, choosing to offer not even so much as a smile. When they reached the hotel doors, he loped a step ahead to open them for her. At the elevator he pressed number two, rode up to her floor with her then walked her down the hall to her door.

She'd slid the key into the lock when he finally cleared his throat. "Wait right here. Let me check things out before you go in."

Not a question but a statement. If she hadn't been so relieved, she might have been miffed. He certainly was a bossy fellow.

The lights flickered on, and Rob stepped inside. He returned to the hallway and gave her a nod. "Looks fine. Just be sure you latch the dead bolt when I leave."

"All right."

"And sleep with your windows closed. I don't like the looks of that fire escape out there. A decent climber would be in your room before you knew what happened."

My, wasn't he the worry wart? She'd been sleeping beside an open window nearly all her life. What point was there in stopping now?

Although she did have to admit she'd locked them last night.

Rob removed the key from the dead bolt and dropped it into her palm. To her surprise he cradled her hand in his.

Their gazes met, and Amalie nearly dropped the key. Something happened in that moment, something she dared not put into words.

Her heart beat a furious rhythm and her mind raced; yet she said nothing.

Rob looked down at his hands then dropped his grip. "Go inside," he said roughly. "I'll wait until I hear the door lock before I leave."

She knew she should do as he asked. If only her feet were willing to take instructions.

He took two steps backward and stuffed his fists into his pockets. "I spoke to Ed. You won't be working the lunch shift tomorrow."

What? Money was too tight to miss a shift. "But I—"

"Not open for discussion." Rob paused to give her a stern look. "Now go to sleep, because I will be back here in the morning at eight. You might have a hard time believing this, but I tend to get cranky when I'm tired." She stepped inside as he'd asked then leaned out to give him a puzzled look. "But where are we going?"

"To find you a suitable place to live." Rob pointed to her shoes, a pair of red pumps that matched her Starlight Grill apron perfectly. "And wear something sensible. We'll be doing a lot of walking."

ঽ

Friday, September 26

At a quarter to eight, Rob parked his truck beneath the vacancy sign and shut off the engine. The ancient V-8 shuddered to a stop, hiccoughing a last gasp before silence reigned.

He'd planned to spend today giving the Chevy a much-needed tune-up, but here he sat with his stomach rumbling and his mind racing. On the seat beside him was today's edition of the paper. *This was a bad idea. I'm sure the Lord wanted me to do this, but maybe I ought to go home now before I get in too deep. I must have misunderstood Him.*

Before he could turn the key, the passenger door flew open.

"Good morning." Amalie Breaux thrust a paper bag in his direction then climbed inside. "I brought breakfast." She pointed up the street. "There's a wonderful little bakery around the corner. They make better biscuits and red-eye gravy than my mama, although I'd never admit that to her."

Rob chuckled despite his mood. "You don't honestly expect me to believe you have biscuits and red-eye gravy in that bag, do you?"

Amalie shrugged. "Of course not. I thought we might try something different." She lifted a pastry out of the bag and inspected it. "They told me this had sausage in it. I hope they're right."

When Rob once more failed to suppress his laughter, Amalie turned in her seat to face him. "What?"

What indeed? How could he tell her that her innocence was the most refreshing thing he'd experienced in ages? That the only thing more pleasant than watching her inspect that pastry was the thought of spending the day with her?

"Why are you looking at me so funny?" She looked down then back up at him. "What is it? Do I have sausage in my teeth?"

Rob shook his head. "I'm sorry. Look—why don't we stop by the diner and fill my thermos with coffee then head out to find you a place to live?"

They spent the morning visiting one advertised apartment after another. By the time they stopped for lunch at the Top Hat Malt Shop across from Hollywood High, the newspaper's classified ad section was covered in circles that had been marked through.

"I'm getting a little worried, Rob," Amalie said as she sipped her chocolate malt at the U-shaped lunch counter. "We've looked at nearly every apartment in the paper and found nothing."

Rather than let on that he agreed, he searched his mind

for a change of topic. "Say, did you know you're sitting on history?" At her confused look he elaborated. "Film history, that is."

"What do you mean?"

"That stool where you're sitting is the very spot where Judy Turner decided to sit one day about five years ago while skipping her typing class."

"Oh?" She looked intrigued but had obviously not made the connection as to whom he referred.

"Well, wouldn't you know it, but Mr. Wilkerson, the owner of the *Hollywood Reporter*, happened in to order a soda. He was famous for drinking twenty colas a day. Did you know that?"

She shook her head, obviously impatient for him to finish his story. As much as he abhorred the Hollywood movie scene, he did love the smile Amalie wore as a result of hearing the tale. And Judy had been a nice kid, at least as far as he remembered, even if she was several years younger than he.

"Well, anyway, there she sat, fifteen-year-old Miss Turner perched right where you are, and along comes this newspaper fellow and asks her if she'd like to be in the movies. You know what she said?"

"No, what?"

"She said she'd have to ask her mother." Rob paused for effect, remembering the tale as he had watched it unfold. "Pretty soon she got a contract with MGM, but she had to pick another name. Care to guess what name she picked?"

Understanding seemed to dawn as her smile grew. "You're teasing me."

"What?"

She rose to look at the stool where she'd been sitting. "This can't be the place where Lana Turner was discovered. That's down the street at Schwab's. Everyone knows that."

Rob grinned. "No, it was here."

Amalie gave him a skeptical look. "How do you know?"

He debated a moment then decided the truth was the least complicated answer. Pointing to the booth in the corner, he shrugged. "I was sitting over there."

eleven

"You're kidding."

"No," Rob said. "I'm serious. As I recall, she wore a blue sweater."

He declined to mention that he, too, was skipping a class, this one senior English literature. Somehow he'd managed to graduate from Hollywood High, though he'd spent more time at the airpark tinkering with planes or in the Top Hat sipping vanilla malts. He decided that information was also off limits to Miss Breaux.

Amalie's jaw dropped, and then a dozen inquiries spilled one after the next from her lips. Rob listened patiently, but without warning he became irritated. For the first time all morning, the woman looked radiant.

The topic of Hollywood had sparked a flame in Amalie Breaux that burned brighter with each question she asked. A flame he certainly hadn't ignited on his own.

So much for assuming this belle of the bayou might see him for who he was and not as the great Roberto Tratelli's only son. *Strange, considering I thought the Lord was behind this friendship.*

Reaching into his wallet, Rob threw three one-dollar bills onto the counter then rose. "Shall we?" he said as he gestured toward the door.

"Yes, well, of course," Amalie stammered. She slid the strap of her handbag over her shoulder and stood to cast one last long look at the famous stool before regarding him with an incredulous look. "You really saw all that? You're not teasing me?"

"Do I look like I'm teasing you?"

77

Amalie ran her hand over the stool then headed for the door. Rob followed a step behind, with conflicting emotions of remorse and relief battling inside.

They made it to the corner of Sunset and Highland before Rob allowed his anger to find words. He pointed across Highland Avenue to Hollywood High School.

"Do you think that the people who go to school there, the same ones who tend to end up on the movie screen, are any better than you or I?"

"What?" Color rushed to her cheeks as her gaze darted between him and the school. "Well, no, I—"

"No, of course they aren't." He paused to ignore a still small voice urging him to cease. "They are normal people who grow up to have lives that include families, pets, and even the occasional trip to the grocery store. They just happen to be part of an industry that is more visible than, say, your average office worker."

He turned to face Sunset. The façade of the Chinese Theater seemed to mock him, so he returned his attention to his companion.

Amalie looked shocked at his outburst. "What's wrong with you?"

What, indeed? To someone not privy to all the facts, his reaction might be met with surprise. Other children of Hollywood, and there were many, would have understood perfectly.

But Amalie Breaux was no child of Hollywood. This Southern beauty admitted to having grown up in the shadow of ancient oaks beside a bayou. Coming to California must have been like entering a foreign country.

Something inside him threatened to melt at the sight of her, so he steeled his resolve.

Better to change the subject than to pursue this one any further. *And while I change the subject, I might as well change our location, too.*

But first he felt he needed to make amends. He may have had good reason for saying what he did, but he was out of line.

Swinging around to the passenger side of the truck, Rob opened the door for Amalie. "Look—I'm sorry for over-reacting, Amalie. Forget I said anything, would you?"

The girl seemed doubtful as she climbed inside. Settling her handbag onto her lap, she reached for the folded newspaper on the seat.

"I don't understand what's wrong with the movie industry. You're always so negative about it." Amalie met his gaze, and her eyes widened. "Say, are you a frustrated actor?"

"What?" For the next five minutes, he proceeded to tell her why he would never set foot inside a Hollywood sound stage. Words like integrity and reality spilled from his mouth along with warnings about what the movie industry did to people, particularly Christians. When he wound down, he noticed his companion was staring at him.

&

"Did you have to go on like that?" Amalie asked. "You could have just said no."

"I merely stated that I have little patience for them," Rob said. "In my opinion actors are often given far more respect than they earn or deserve."

"As I said, Rob, you could have just said no."

Amalie gave Rob a sideways glance then returned her concentration to the newspaper in her lap. As she read the last two remaining apartment ads, her mind wandered to the strange conclusion to today's lunch. First he told her a fascinating tale; then he flew off the handle when she acted interested in his story.

Men. Who would ever understand them?

Any normal person would have managed to go from the beginning of a story about Lana Turner to the end of it with-out changing from a nice fellow to a real—a real what? She couldn't think of a suitable word.

"Do you want to try the place on Franklin first or the one on Cory?"

She glanced in his direction and shrugged. "Whichever you think best," she said. "I'm still learning the area."

"Of course." He braked at the light on Sunset. "Cory," he said, "and then Franklin."

"All right."

He reached over to touch her hand. "Look, Amalie. I'm really sorry. It's just that this movie thing, well, sometimes it gets to me that people see it as something it's not."

The sincerely penitent look on Rob's face saved him. Amalie sighed then managed a weak smile. "As I said before, you sound like someone who knows a lot about the film industry. As for me, all I know is what I read in the screen magazines, but I aim to learn."

Rob banged his fist on the steering wheel as the light turned green. "See, that's what I'm talking about. Here you are, green as it gets, and depending on magazines to teach you how to avoid the pitfalls of Hollywood." He gave her a long look at the next light. "It doesn't work like that, Amalie. A girl like you will get eaten up by this town in no time if you're not careful."

"Rob," Amalie said softly, "are you a Christian?"

He looked surprised, but he nodded. "Yes, since I was nine. Why?"

"Have you ever thought God was telling you to do something you weren't prepared to do? I mean, something that seemed so far out of your normal routine that you were doing it only because you believed He was leading you to do it?"

"Amalie, you have no idea." He paused, obviously realizing her confusion. "The answer is, yes, I believe He has. In fact, I'm only here right now because I felt He wanted me here."

Oh? Interesting.

Rob made a few turns; then Cory Street loomed ahead. "Why do you ask?" he said as he signaled to turn.

"Because I believe I'm here at the Lord's leading, too." He shook his head as if to disagree, and she shrugged. "All right, go ahead and think what you want. Yes, I want to be a star. In fact, I left my home and family to make that dream come true, but you know what?"

"What?"

"I prayed before I got on that bus, and I've been praying every day since."

Rob slowed to a stop in front of a down-at-the-heels apartment complex with a faded "FOR RENT" sign. He turned to face her. "Praying for what, Amalie? That God will make you rich and famous?"

"No, actually, that's not it at all." She paused to look up at the nightmare of a building that could become her second home. "I pray that He will keep me from becoming all of that if it's not His will."

Rob climbed out of the truck and walked around to the other side to open Amalie's door. "What's the difference?" he asked. "One's the same as the other in my book."

"The difference, Rob, is that I know I could be a star." Eyes narrowed, she stopped to stare at Rob. "But I don't want it if that's not what His best is."

The shocked look on his face matched hers when she opened the door to the only vacant apartment in the building. Before she could comment, Rob led her back to the truck and helped her inside.

"Franklin?" he asked.

"Franklin," she answered.

&

Saturday, September 27

The last apartment she looked at was the one she settled into the next day. With little required in the way of moving, Amalie was able to take the city bus from the hotel to her apartment on Franklin Street with only her suitcase and a pasteboard box. Inside the box, tucked amongst the various foodstuffs and kitchen items and hidden beneath her pillow and quilt from home, was a writing pad with a half-finished letter.

Dated two days ago, the letter contained a glowing description of Hollywood and the casting call she would attend. "Better to start over and not mention that," she said as she wadded the letter into a ball and tossed it into the trash can.

Three drafts later, she settled on a note stating that she'd moved to an apartment with a view and would write soon. She didn't say the view was of a brick wall.

At least this neighborhood was nice, and the bus stopped only steps from her door. To top it off, the landlord told her the actor Ronald Reagan had only recently moved out of an apartment in the building. Now *that* she could mention in a letter home.

Then there was Rob. Papa would like him, of that she felt sure.

A knock at the door made her jump. When she opened it and found Rob standing there, she smiled.

He thrust a handful of flowers in her direction. "A house-warming gift," he said.

"Thank you," she said. "Won't you come in?"

"Actually I was hoping you would go out," he said. "With me, that is."

twelve

Amalie's first inclination was to say no. Too many reasons to stay home and away from any further involvement with Rob stood between her and good sense, and yet out she went. Perhaps it was Rob's promise to show her the best of Hollywood, or maybe it was the fear that if she didn't go she might miss something interesting.

She glanced at the clock. "I'm working the evening shift so I don't see how we could possibly—"

"Don't worry about it," Rob said with an impish grin. "I promise to show you all of Hollywood that's worth seeing *and* have you back in time to make your shift. What do you say? Are you game?"

Amalie gave him a sideways look. "What happened to that guy from yesterday? The grumpy one?"

He paused and seemed to consider the question. A look crossed his face, but she couldn't decide what it meant.

Leaning against the door frame, Rob crossed his hands over his chest. His steady gaze met hers. "I was way off base, Amalie. I hope you can forgive me."

"Of course."

"As of today I'm a new man. I promise."

Amalie giggled. "I believe you, Rob. It's all right."

"I don't want to use this as an excuse for my rudeness. There is no excuse." He paused. "See, there are things about me you don't know." Rob turned his attention to studying the backs of his hands. "Things that give me a natural inclination to dislike certain aspects of the motion picture business—though as I said, that does not give me an excuse to act as I did."

He offered no further explanation. Amalie would like to have pressed the point, but she didn't. Rather, she considered the other choices she had for passing the day until five o'clock. An empty pantry in want of filling and a pasteboard box that needed taking to the trash bin were the only things on her agenda.

That and writing a real letter home.

A letter that contained her new address.

Amalie gulped, her decision made. "I hope you realize you are taking me away from important activities."

Rob's grin deepened as his gaze swept the room. "Like what? Consulting with your decorator?"

"Very funny. Now tell me where we're going so I can dress appropriately."

"Well, now," he said slowly, "I think you look fine the way you are."

Amalie looked down at her dungarees and plaid top, buttoned up to the neck and tied at the waist. She'd taken the clothes off the line back in Latagnier as a last-minute grab for extra outfits for her trip to California. When her little brother discovered his favorite fishing outfit was gone, he'd likely had a fit.

Until this moment she hadn't realized she was wearing it in front of Rob.

"Oh, no, I never meant to be seen in this. I can't."

Rob took her hand and spun her around. "Amalie Breaux, you look incredible. I don't know when I've ever seen denim and plaid worn more properly. Now fetch your house key. We have some stars to see."

"Stars?" Her heart soared, but she tempered her expression. "Are you sure?"

"Trust me. These are stars that both of us can appreciate." Rob took a step backward into the hall and jangled his keys. "So are you coming or what?"

As she settled into the truck next to him a few minutes later, she smiled. "Where to?"

"I thought I'd show you where the biggest star in Hollywood hangs out first." Another glance, another grin. "See, I told you I am mending my ways."

They headed down Franklin toward the city's outskirts. Up ahead a large star loomed atop a sign directing customers to a newly built miniature golf course.

From where she sat, it appeared to be hanging over the words HOLLYWOOD STARLAND MINIATURE GOLF.

"This is where the biggest star in Hollywood hangs out?" When Rob slowed the truck and signaled to turn in, Amalie gave him a playful shove. "You're joking, right?"

Rob shook his head. "I told you I'd take you to see the stars in Hollywood, and there's the biggest one of the bunch, at least as far as I know. Just wait until you see what I have planned next."

"I'm afraid to ask."

"Then don't."

Somewhere between putt-putt golf at the Hollywood Starland and choosing a sorrel gelding named Big Star to ride through Griffith Park, Amalie fell in love, first with Hollywood and then with Rob Cantoni.

It could have been the beautiful day, or maybe it was the horse ride in the sheltering confines of the park. But, Amalie decided, it could possibly be the leading of the Lord.

She wouldn't have chosen such an unlikely fellow on her own. After all, he did have his grumpy side.

But something about the fry cook held her heart captive.

He was the first man Amalie thought might pass muster with Papa, and he seemed to care for her safety more than most men she'd been around. Why, the man had a fit when she tried to ride off without him.

Slowing her mare to a trot, she allowed him to catch up to

her. "You don't ride horses much, do you, Rob?"

Rob shook his head and adjusted his position in the saddle. "I had hoped you wouldn't notice."

They rode side by side over the rise and back toward the barn to return the horses. "Are you hungry?" he asked as they left the barn.

She was ravenous. "A little," she said.

"Good." Rob gestured to the bed of the truck where a bucket stuffed with a piece of silky pale cloth sat. "I brought lunch."

"Oh." She didn't dare to ask what sort of lunch might warrant being stuffed into a bucket. Whatever it was, she would be polite.

Minutes later they drove under a large wood framed arch with the inscription 4-STAR RANCH emblazoned in black iron letters and large iron stars on either side. Very large stars. Lots of them.

"Cute," she said as she pointed to the arch. "Another place with big stars."

He shrugged. "I didn't lie. There they are."

The truck bounced along a dirt road until Rob brought it to a halt at the edge of an orange grove. Just ahead was a small gazebo tucked amongst the trees.

Rob climbed out and retrieved the bucket. "Ready?" he asked.

"Sure." His enthusiasm worked on her concern until she arrived at the little table in the gazebo ready to devour whatever the container held.

Rob set the bucket down on the bench and gave her a repentant look. "I have to confess that I had a little help with lunch. If it were left up to me, peanut butter sandwiches would be in here." He paused. "I packed it myself though, so please forgive the fact that I had to use a piece of parachute as a tablecloth. That's all I had on hand."

"Dare I ask," she said slowly, "but how is it you had parachutes on hand?"

"I'm a man of many mysteries," he said with a wicked grin, "chief among them my access to airplane parts." He shrugged. "Actually my uncle and I are restoring a plane. Since it doesn't fly yet, I haven't repacked the parachutes."

Removing the cloth with a flourish, he positioned it on the table then took out foil-wrapped packets from inside. Under the packets were two sets of silverware and a pair of napkins. He unfolded Amalie's and set it in her lap then dashed around the table to sit across from her.

"Oh, wait!" Rob jumped up and raced back to the truck to dig behind the seat. He emerged from the vehicle with a thermos in one hand and two tin cups in the other. "I forgot the bubbly."

Amalie frowned. "Rob, I don't drink."

"Neither do I." Her host winked as he opened the thermos. "But there's nothing better than ice cold club soda with a twist of fresh orange. All the stars love it."

❧

"Stop it, Rob."

Amalie's giggle was adorable. So was the way she scrunched up her nose when the bubbles from the club soda teased it. When she took a sip of the orange-flavored drink he found himself watching her lips touch the tin cup and then as she swallowed.

Come to your senses, Tratelli. You're mooning over the woman like a lovesick pup.

"Let's see what's in here, shall we?" Unless Cook misheard, there should be roasted chicken, red grapes, a fresh loaf of rye bread, and two white-chocolate raspberry tarts.

"Oh," she said softly as he unwrapped the last of the packets and set them in the center of the table.

"What? Is something wrong?" Rob looked down at the spread then back at his guest. "You don't like chicken?" He rose. "What do you like? Tell me, and I'll have—that is, I'll go and get it. I mean, well, you know what I mean."

"No, I mean, yes." Amalie sighed. "What I mean is, I love chicken. It's just that this is so. . ." She met his gaze with a look of wonder. "It's lovely."

He exhaled the breath he hadn't realized he'd been holding. "Oh, good. You had me worried."

Amalie popped a grape in her mouth and savored it before finally swallowing. "Incredible," she said. "Absolutely incredible."

Rob looked into the wide eyes of Amalie Breaux and fell in love all over again. Not simple infatuation or that silly junior-high crush stuff.

"Yes," Rob said slowly, "you are." He cleared his throat. "I mean, it is, isn't it? Here." Somehow he managed to thrust a chicken leg in her direction. "Try this."

If his companion noticed his shaking hand, she had the decency not to mention it. "So, Rob," she said between bites, "if you could do anything for a living, what would it be?"

Her innocent expression belied the seriousness of the question. "Well, I know I don't want to fry burgers."

The wind danced past and shook the trees, lifting the corners of the makeshift tablecloth. "Somehow I didn't think so." Amalie gave him an appraising look. "Let me see if I can guess. It's not fry cook, and I'm thinking you probably don't want to be a chef." She glanced at the parachute-turned-tablecloth then up at him. "Pilot, perhaps?"

"Bingo," he said as he tore off a piece of bread and popped it in his mouth.

As she squeezed more orange juice into her cup, she seemed to be pondering something. Finally she came out with it.

"I think you should be one then."

The bite of bread went down with difficulty. "One what?"

"A pilot. I think you should be one. If that's what God

is calling you to do, then you must heed the call, even if it means making difficult choices."

Amalie looked so satisfied with herself that he hated to burst her bubble. Still, he had to say something.

"You know there's a war on," he said. Simple statement, not-so-simple meaning.

"Yes." She studied the ceiling of the gazebo then turned her attention to him. "Is that what's stopping you? From flying?"

He gave the question the thought it deserved. "That's part of it," he finally said.

"And the rest of it?"

Amalie's direct look unnerved him. "And the rest of it is that my parents are adamantly opposed to my signing up to fly for this country or any other."

"Go on," she said.

"There's nothing else to say. I made a promise to them, and I intend to keep it."

Her fingers smoothed a dark hair away from her face. "If it's not too bold, might you tell me what that promise was?"

Did he mind? Oh, why not? He'd already spilled much more than he intended.

"I agreed not to join up unless the war comes to our shores." He lifted a piece of chicken to his lips then thought better of it and set it back on the foil. "It's a difficult promise to keep, I'll tell you that much. When I read the papers and hear how my father's homeland has been. . .destroyed, it's difficult to stand by. I know the Lord asks us to honor our parents, but doesn't He also want us to keep the world safe for His kingdom?"

Rob paused and waved away the unpleasant topic with a sweep of his hand. No sense ruining a pleasant day with such a disagreeable topic. Someday the war would come, and he would fly. Until then he could only bide his time and enjoy moments like this one.

"Forgive me, Amalie. I'm not going to ruin our lunch with this kind of talk."

"I brought it up," she said.

"No, you asked what I would do if I could do anything. You know, I have a good answer for that. You see, my uncle and I are working on a plane that I hope to be the first of a fleet of domestic and international delivery carriers." He chuckled. "It's a lofty dream, but I hope someday to give the boys at the post office some serious competition for air deliveries."

"Really?" She shook her head. "I don't think I could ever be brave enough to go up in one of those contraptions. It doesn't even seem as if it should go up in the air."

"Simple science, Amalie," he said. "Drag and lift."

Again she shook her head. "Here's how I look at it. If I can't take this grape and throw it into the air and expect it to fly, then why should I expect something that weighs more than that truck over there to do it?"

"You really want to know how it works?"

She leaned forward and rested her elbows on the table, cradling her chin in her hands. "Go ahead and try to explain it so I can understand. I have to warn you—science was never my best subject."

By the time he escorted her to the truck, he'd managed to impart the basics of airplane engines and the science behind their ability to lift off the ground and maintain height. The bayou beauty seemed to take it all in, sort it out, and manage to look impressed. Whether she understood a word he said didn't matter at that moment, for he'd managed to capture and hold her attention.

That in itself was reward enough to see him through the ride home and the walk to her door.

"Thank you for a lovely day, Rob," she said as she turned to look into his eyes. Until that moment he hadn't given a thought to how tall she was. What hadn't slipped his mind was how beautiful she was.

"My pleasure." He watched her grin grow into a smile. "What's so funny?"

She seemed reluctant to respond. "It's just that, well, I didn't expect to be treated so—"

"Nice?"

"Yes," Amalie said softly. "Nice, that's it."

"It's easy to be nice to you, Amalie. I like you a lot"

She laughed out loud. "I like you, too," she said. "A lot."

If he hadn't been raised a gentleman, he might have kissed her right then. Then another thought dawned. This beautiful woman, the one encouraging him to follow his dreams without regard to the difficulties they might impose, was the same woman who'd spent Thursday afternoon sitting in a casting call to become a movie star.

It was all he could do not to turn and run. The only thing keeping him rooted in place was the odd thought that the Lord wanted him right where he was.

Well, as long as I'm standing here. . .I'm going to kiss her. Unless You tell me not to. But the Lord immediately spoke a clear and definite *Not yet* into his ear before he could take the first step toward her.

A few minutes later, he'd given her a hug and a quick hand-shake and bolted to the truck. *From now on it's friendship only with Miss Breaux.*

But as soon as he had the thought he dismissed it. As long as he worked at the Starlight Grill, he would be trying to balance his desire to wait on the Lord with wanting to spend more time away from the diner with Amalie Breaux.

"Oh, why not?" he muttered. "Lord, until You let me know otherwise, I hope to keep having days like today with Amalie. Who knows? Maybe she will change her mind about this movie star stuff."

Then will you tell her who you really are?

"Ouch."

He threw the truck into gear and pulled away from the curb. "I ought to do that pretty soon, shouldn't I?"

Even though the Lord didn't answer, Rob knew what His response would be.

Yes.

thirteen

Theophile Breaux sat at the kitchen table with the *New Iberia Daily Leader* spread across his wife's flowered tablecloth. The headlines screamed war, declaring the United States would soon be pulled into action. How, the columnist declared, could the greatest country in the world stand idly by when innocent people were losing their freedom and their lives?

"How, indeed?"

Am I not guilty of doing the same thing with my daughter? Amalie has been gone nigh on three months, and I haven't moved a finger to find her and bring her home. Oh, sure, I raised a ruckus with old Gip Gonsulin when he admitted to driving her into town, and I spread the word I was looking to get her back home, but what did I really do to fetch her back? Maybe it's time to buy a bus ticket to California.

Maybe I need to do something other than stand idly by.

And then there's this awful war. What will become of our sons? Ernest, who is too old to go but will most likely enlist all the same, and the young ones—they will go for sure. And Mathilde's Nicolas and Angie's Doctor Jeff, what will they do?

"What's it all coming to?"

"What's that, Theo? You talking to the newspaper again, sweetheart?"

He looked up to see his wife standing on the other side of the screen door pulling off her gardening gloves. Up to her elbows in weeding with bits of Spanish moss in her hair and

93

splotches of mud splashed across her apron, Clothilde Breaux was still the prettiest thing he'd ever laid eyes on.

Theo rose to tell her so then followed her gaze to the cloud coming up the dirt road. "A car," he said under his breath. He looked at Cleo, and a single thought passed between them.

Amalie.

As the vehicle drew nearer, Theo made out the familiar shape of the mail truck. "It's Wednesday, *cher*," he said, masking his disappointment with a firm voice. "Maybe there's something from. . ."

He couldn't say it. Cleo, God bless her, who made it her business to complete as many sentences as she could for him, remained silent as well.

The postman hollered a greeting, and Theo responded. Three envelopes and a magazine later, the truck roared back the same way it came. Theo strolled back inside and laid the mail atop the paper.

"Anything?" Cleo called. "I kind of hoped she'd be back for Thanksgiving."

Looking over his shoulder to see his wife standing in the doorway, Theo reached for the topmost envelope. Heedless of the mud on her boots, she tracked a path toward him and the envelope he held.

"Is it from my baby?" Cleo whispered. "Is she coming home?"

He handed it to her without comment. Just like the others, it bore no return address. No doubt there would be a page or two of fancy talk about what movie she was going to try out for next and why she missed out on getting a part in the last one. She wrote one regular as clockwork on the first day of every month. Generally the letter came on the Wednesday mail route, but sometimes the postman skipped a week.

It broke his heart that his baby girl was out there on the other side of creation doing who knew what. But what hurt most was the way her mama cried at night, heaving silent sobs into her pillow when she thought he was asleep.

A man could go hoarse faking snoring so that his woman could get her weeping done in peace. He should know; it happened at least once a week.

Theo got halfway to his thinking spot on the bayou before he let loose with his complaints to the Lord. "Why can't You just make her come home, Father? Is nothing too hard for You? Your book says it is not. Give this father his daughter back. Whatever she's done, I don't care. Just bring her home. No questions asked."

No questions asked? You will love her no matter what she's done?

When the Father brought his words back to him, Theo stopped but finally managed to say, "Yes, Lord, no matter what."

Falling to his knees where he was, Theo felt soft earth give way and mud soak into his pants legs. He didn't care. Something much bigger than a pair of soiled trousers was at stake here.

Something like the return of his daughter.

"Lord, I'll stay here all day in this mud if You will just send my Amalie home. Or You know what? You tell me where she is, and I'll go get her. Indeed I will."

And that's where he was when Cleo found him, knee-deep in mud and tears streaming down his face. Rather than fuss or worry, Cleo kicked off her good shoes and landed on her knees beside him. "What are we praying for, husband?"

He swiped at his face with his shirtsleeve then kissed the top of her head. "Amalie, *cher*. The Lord, He needs to bring her home."

Cleo nodded and entwined her hand with his. "*Oui*," she said softly. "And may He act quickly." She nudged his shoulder. "And, Theo, please let's pray for our boys. I'm just a woman, but I know a thing or two about what's going on in the world outside my kitchen. I love my boys, but if they must give their lives to their country, would you pray for their safety?"

"*Oui*," he said through his tightened throat. "These times, *cher*, are changing."

"Oh, yes," Cleo said as she reached to clasp her hand in his. "But our Lord, He never changes. If He can give up His Son for the good of others, then who are we to refuse ours?"

&

Wednesday, November 5
Hollywood, California

"Where are you tonight, Amalie?" Rob smiled. "I know you're not here."

Amalie shook her head and stepped back from the telescope. "I'm sorry. What did you say?"

Rob turned her to face him. "I said that although we're here atop the mountain with the telescope on this incredibly clear night in the middle of a meteor shower, you don't seem to be able to see a single star."

"Story of my life," Amalie muttered, looking away.

Behind her the sky glittered with a million pinpricks of light while below in the valley the city shimmered. Only the place beneath their feet and the hills to their right and left seemed dark, a counterpoint to the glory of God's nighttime creation.

On good days Rob could scarcely take it all in. Tonight, however, he'd barely given it a second glance. His concern and his attention lay with Amalie.

So did his heart.

He'd planned all week for this night, poring over the weather forecasts and praying for good weather and God's blessing. Too bad he hadn't prayed for Amalie's good humor.

"All right, that's it." Rob led her to a low-slung boulder and settled her there, wrapping the blanket he'd brought around her shoulders. "Now are you going to tell me what's wrong, or do I have to pry it out of you with torture?"

She looked away and protested her innocence. Rob sat beside her and leaned in her direction, chuckling despite the dread welling in his gut. "I should warn you. I have my ways of making people talk."

"Like what?"

"Like, oh, I don't know." He paused. "Look—I care deeply for you, Amalie, and I don't want to see you this way. Please tell me what's wrong."

"I can't. Not tonight, Rob."

He shrugged beneath the blanket and let her rest her head on his shoulder. Within minutes, his heart swelled with a peace and joy he'd never expected to find. A mountaintop experience, his father would call it.

And it was happening atop a mountain.

He leaned over and kissed Amalie.

&

What a kiss.

Suddenly it was as if the Lord had painted each star into the sky just for her then tossed a meteor or two in for good measure. Fireworks, yes, but more. . .deeper. . .familiar and yet new and different.

So quickly, so easily, to turn her spirits from low to high. What a puzzle. What power this man held.

Amalie's heart raced as fast as her thoughts. When she finally met his gaze, she could feel the heat spreading across her cheeks.

Her first kiss. What a glorious place for it.

"Now that's better."

She blinked but could find no words. Snuggling into Rob's embrace, she watched the Lord entertain them with falling stars and knew she, too, was falling—in love.

"Rob?" she whispered.

"Um-hum," came his soft reply.

"This is my favorite star date of all."

He wrapped his arm around her waist and drew her close. "I agree," he said.

fourteen

Even though the first of December lay weeks ahead, Amalie had already begun her monthly letter home. She'd started it last night after work, intending to tell Mama and Papa all about the upcoming Thanksgiving feast at the Starlight Grill for those down on their luck. Rob had come up with the idea, but to include that she would have to tell them about Rob.

And what was there to say? That she was madly, hopelessly in love with a man they'd never met?

Torn between needing to stay and wanting to go made a girl feel dizzy. But then so did spending time with Rob. Last Friday on their weekly "star date"—this time to the Griffith Observatory—she'd finally told him of the homesickness that had plagued her for the last week, blaming it on the arrival of an early winter and the rapid approach of Thanksgiving.

Even now as she paused, pencil hovering inches from the page, she could hear his response.

"Go home, then, Amalie, but not without me."

Not without him.

She hadn't known how to respond then, but today she knew in her heart what to say. "Come with me then," she whispered. "Come and meet Mama and Papa." She paused, and an idea dawned, an idea so perfect she chided herself for not thinking of it before now.

She would bring Rob home to Latagnier for Christmas.

Amalie rose and dropped the pencil then watched it roll

across the table and fall. Thanks to the uneven floor, the pencil jolted to a stop beside her bare foot. She picked it up and jotted a note without sitting down, a word of caution to her parents that she might grace them with a Christmas visit.

She rose to don her "casting call dress," a pretty chiffon number with bows and buttons. "Another day, another opportunity to get turned down by a studio."

Using every day off she had, Amalie had managed to be turned down by every major studio in town. Auditions were always first on the list, but the last job she'd been refused was a janitor's position at Imperial Studios.

"Now *that* is the height of desperation."

At least Rob didn't know about that one. He'd put up with her insistence on pursuing her acting dreams, but she knew he had reservations. It was enough that he'd finally kissed her. Any disagreements they had paled in comparison to the memory of their first kiss.

And their second.

And every one of the kisses she'd received since then.

Ever the gentleman, Rob limited himself to one good-night kiss each day, promising that any more might bring about a speedy trip down a slippery slope. While she admired his chivalrous restraint, her heart often ached for more.

Funny how, though she had an audition this afternoon, her date with Rob tonight looked like the one bright spot in the day. Maybe she would skip the audition.

Just this once.

She slipped her audition dress back onto the hanger and put it away.

ça

Rob let himself into the Starlight Grill then locked the door behind him. The lunch rush was still several hours away, but his work would begin the moment he walked into the kitchen. He shrugged out of his coat and hung it on the rack beside the door then stopped in his tracks.

Had Ed left the kitchen light on again?

And what was that smell? If he didn't know better he would think someone was frying bacon.

Easing up to the kitchen door, he peered inside. Tillie Rush stood at the stove, a smile on her face and a flamboyant paisley scarf covering her head.

"Hello, there, handsome," she said with a wink. "I said to myself, 'Tillie, what's a girl got to do to get a decent BLT?' And you know what I figured out?"

Rob grinned and shook his head. "What's that?"

"Just as Judy Garland said, 'There's no place like home.'"

Enveloping Tillie in a bear hug took seconds. Letting her go a little longer. "Welcome home, Tillie," he said.

"It's good to be here." She gestured to the dining room then built two BLTs from the ingredients on the sideboard. "What say you and me go have us a getting-reacquainted talk?"

"Sounds good."

"I hear you're in love," she said when he'd settled across from her in the booth.

"You don't mince words, do you?"

Her eyes narrowed. "I'm too old to waste time. So what's the story?"

"The story." He paused to decide what parts of the story to tell and what to leave out. "Let's see. I met a great gal named Amalie. She's from Louisiana. You'll meet her tomorrow when she works the breakfast shift."

"And?"

"And I like her a lot. Love her, maybe."

"But?"

"But what, Tillie?"

"But what's the catch? If she's so great and you care for her, what's the problem?" She nibbled at the corner of her sandwich then set it on her plate. "And don't give me the sanitized version."

"She wants to be an actress."

Tillie took in the statement and appeared to be weighing it. "And you figured she will end up like your cousin Helena."

"No. . .yes. . .oh, I don't know." Rob met her even stare. "Maybe," he finally said as he exhaled.

She reached across the table to take his hand in hers. "Honey, I haven't told you where I've been, and you have the good manners not to ask. See, I didn't just take a trip on a whim. The Lord, He told me, 'Tillie, you need a rest. Give Rob the keys to the place and go have an adventure.' So off I went."

"Is that right?"

"It is, and someday I'll tell you all about it. But here's the thing." She broke off a piece of bacon and savored it. "When my adventure was over, He let me know that, too. 'Tillie,' He said, 'Get yourself on home. I've got something new for Rob.' So here I am."

"It's good to have you back." Truly it was, for now he wouldn't have to hear Uncle Gio complain about the hours Rob spent at the diner.

"So what is it the Lord has for you? Is it this gal?"

He gave the question some thought before deciding he had no answer. What he hoped and what he knew were two different things. Before he could say so, Tillie rose to retrieve an oversize black beaded handbag from behind the counter.

"Well, now," Tillie said as she settled once again into the booth, "I am a bit disappointed. I thought you would be able to tell me why I was supposed to give you this." She lifted a thick brown envelope out of her handbag and pushed it toward him across the table.

Lifting the seal, he caught sight of the envelope's contents: a neat stack of hundred-dollar bills. Closing it quickly, he slid the envelope back toward her.

"I can't take this," he said, "although I will be forever grateful that you thought enough of me to want to give it."

His statement did not seem to surprise her. "Oh, honey, the Lord told me you were stubborn, but He didn't tell me *how* stubborn. That's payment for all the help you've been to me since I flew the coop."

"Really, Tillie, I—"

"You kept the place running, even appointing Ed to manage it. I like that about you, honey. You never try to steal the glory. That's why I don't want you to miss out on whatever the Lord's intending you to do with this."

"But what about Ed? He did all the hard work. I just flipped burgers and took out the trash."

Tillie's smile lit her entire face. "Don't you worry about your cousin Eduardo. I've got an envelope for him, too." She lifted a much thinner version of his envelope out of her handbag. "I'll bet you're thinking Ed's getting the poor end of the deal."

"The thought occurred to me."

Tillie leaned forward then looked first to her right and then to her left before turning her attention back to Rob. "Ed's getting the diner." She thumped the envelope then stuffed it back into her purse. "That there's the deed."

"But why?"

"Because I'm supposed to. Beyond that it's none of your business."

Before Rob could take it all in, Tillie grasped his hand again. "Rob, you don't have to tell me what you're planning to do with the money. Just tell me you plan to ask the Lord."

"Oh, that I will do." But as he spoke the words a thought landed on his heart and took hold. *If that envelope held even half the amount he suspected, he had just found the capital to begin the aviation business he'd been dreaming of.*

"Amalie," he whispered. "I need to tell Amalie."

"Tell Amalie what?"

Rob looked up to see her standing at the door. He rose to greet her with a kiss on the cheek then made the introductions.

"So pleased to finally make your acquaintance, Miss Tillie," Amalie said. "Rob and Ed speak of you kindly and with great frequency. The only thing that puzzles me is that you are much younger than I expected."

Tillie turned to grin at Rob. "Oh, I like her. I like her a lot."

Rob caught Amalie's hand and held it. "So do I," he said as he nudged Amalie. "A lot." He paused to check his watch. "Say, weren't you supposed to be somewhere about now?"

Amalie met his gaze with a twinkle in her eyes. "There's no place I would rather be right this minute than where I am. There's always tomorrow for everything else."

Tillie stood and reached for her handbag. "I must be going. But, first, do you mind if I borrow your young lady for a moment?"

When Amalie returned she was silent but smiling and refused to disclose the subject of her conversation with Tillie. She wore that same smile through the lunch shift and later at the Brown Derby where they dined on steak.

Amalie seemed to care deeply for him. If only Rob knew for sure that she would continue to feel the same once she learned the truth about his background.

Worse, if she seemed as swayed by his famous father's Hollywood connections, how would he react? Would he still love Amalie Breaux even if she asked him to use his father as a means to further her career?

If onlys continued to plague him until he could barely pay attention. Leaning back against the brown velvet cushions of the booth, Rob prayed for the right words to use to spill his secret, the words ordained by the Father to keep him from losing the love of his life.

The other piece of news, the fact that he'd spoken to Uncle Gio and decided to give wings, literally, to his dream of an aviation business by using Tillie's gift, would be much easier to break to her. The deception, however, bore hard on his heart and seared his mind.

Finally he dashed into the men's room to splash cold water on his face. Staring into his own eyes reflected in the ornate mirror, he came to a single realization: He served a God of truth and mercy.

All Rob could think to do was tell Amalie the truth and pray for mercy. When he returned to the table he kissed her cheek.

"What's wrong, Rob?" Amalie frowned. "Are you still worried about why I showed up for the lunch shift?"

Rob shook his head. "No, I'm glad you got to meet Tillie. And I'm always glad to see you. You know that."

She ducked her head and studied the red damask tablecloth. "As I told you earlier, I wanted to see you. The other thing didn't seem as important today."

The other thing. Oh, I like the sound of this. Soon she will forget about making movies altogether.

Now to straighten out the mess with his last name.

He reached for her hand and entwined his fingers with hers. "Amalie, I need to tell you something. It's important. Actually I need to tell you a couple of things."

Her look of alarm caught him by surprise. "No, honey, don't worry. It's not awful. At least I don't think it is." But he wondered if Amalie would disagree.

Still, the truth was the truth, and there was power in telling it—even if the news was a bit late in coming.

"First of all, I'm leaving the diner."

Her frown deepened. "Why? Have I done something wrong?"

"Oh, no, sweetheart," he said with a chuckle. "You've done everything right. It's just that I've been given the opportunity to follow my dreams."

"Tillie's gift?"

"Yes," Rob said. "I spoke to Uncle Gio, and we're going forward with our plans for the aviation company."

"I'm so happy for you, Rob. This is your dream come true."

He paused. "I thought I would run the name by you to see what you thought."

"All right. What is it?"

"Star Aviation," he said with a grin. "Appropriately named after our weekly dates. Now we can start going there instead of looking for other stars."

Amalie giggled and gave him a playful shove. "As for those weekly dates, we will have to talk about whether your office counts as an actual dating spot. Although I do like that you named it for our dates."

She took that well enough. Now for the other piece of news. "Amalie?"

"Yes?"

"Remember way back when you first met Ed and me? The day Ed hired you?"

She nodded.

"Well, I don't know if you recall this, but Ed introduced me as his cousin Rob." He paused to allow her a moment to consider his statement. "Just Rob. Nothing more. Do you remember?"

Amalie creased her brow as she seemed to be considering the question. "Yes, I think I remember that. Why?"

"Well, honey, at that time you knew Ed's last name was Cantoni, right? I mean, Ed told you that, didn't he?"

Her "yes" was slow in coming. "Why, Rob?" she asked much faster.

"Well, you see, I—"

"Robbie, boy, is that you?"

Rob looked up to see someone familiar standing at their table. Far too familiar. He glanced at Amalie and noticed that all the color had drained from her face.

"Carole, come see who's here. It's Robbie." He clasped Rob's hand then stood back to give him an appraising look. "How long's it been—six months? I haven't played a decent round of golf since I met you and your father. Where have you been?"

"Right here in Hollywood, actually."

Amalie's lips began to move, but no sound came out. Finally she managed a weak, "Oh."

"Amalie, honey," Rob said with a smile he hoped would pass muster. "Say hello to Clark Gable. Mr. Gable, this is my friend Amalie Breaux."

"Pleased to meet you," he said, and his famous wife repeated the sentiment. A few minutes of small talk and a promise to get together soon, and the couple made a quiet exit out the side entrance.

Rob knew, however, that his own exit would be more spectacular. As soon as Amalie could regain her power of speech, she was sure to let him have it.

"Check, please!"

fifteen

"Clark Gable and Carole Lombard." Amalie stood beneath the awning of the Brown Derby watching the rain beat down around her and on the snarl of traffic on Wilshire Boulevard. "Clark Gable called you Robbie and asked about your father, and Carole Lombard asked for your mother's sweet potato pie recipe."

Oh, boy. He was in big trouble.

Well, it's not as if the Lord didn't warn me. I should have confessed long before now.

"Yes, well, how about that?" he said quickly. "It's pouring out here so let me go get the truck. You stay put."

She pulled on her gloves and reached for his hand. "Rob, how does Clark Gable know you?"

He extricated himself from her grip and stepped out into the downpour with only his overcoat for cover. "Be right back," he called as the first icy pellets of November rain slashed at his face and wiggled a cold trail down his back.

Miserable as he felt, it was still preferable to standing in the heat of Amalie's questioning gaze.

As he stomped through puddles to retrieve his vehicle, Rob sorted through several defenses—from total silence to complete confession. While he could find merit in each option, the common denominator was truth. He had to tell her the truth.

He was thankful she accepted his silence without comment on the ride back to Franklin Avenue. He walked her to her door, and then, departing from routine, he grasped her hand and touched her fingers to his lips.

"I'm sure you have questions for me."

She looked into his eyes and nodded slowly. "How does a pilot and a fry cook at the Starlight Grill end up playing golf with Clark Gable?"

Good question. Bad answer. "I guess you could say I haven't told you everything about my family."

"Actually you haven't told me anything, now that I think of it." When he loosened his grip, Amalie reached up to swipe at the raindrops decorating his cheek. "You're soaked. You'll catch your death out here."

Rob shrugged. Somewhere between the parking lot of the Brown Derby and the sidewalk leading to Amalie's apartment he'd grown numb. "I'd be glad to spill my guts for a hot cup of coffee and a dry towel."

An eternity passed while Amalie seemed to consider his offer. Meanwhile, rain beat down on the sidewalk inches away, dotting his already damp pants legs and soaking his skin to the bone.

If he made it through tonight without losing Amalie, he'd be thrilled. Escaping with his health, now that seemed to be another matter altogether.

He sneezed. "Maybe I should go," he said.

&

Amalie almost let him go. Rob had already turned up the collar on his overcoat and prepared to dart out toward the truck when she got off her high horse and relented. Sure, the guy had obviously left a few things out of his biography, but she'd never find out what they were by giving him the cold shoulder.

"Rob." When he turned around she forced a pleasant tone. "I'm going to take you up on that offer of the truth. Don't disappoint me."

Ten minutes later, Rob sat at the kitchen table bundled up in a blanket with a mug of strong black coffee in his hands.

Amalie poured half a cup for herself then settled across from him, averting her gaze.

"Too much doesn't add up, Rob. I need some answers."

"I know, and I'm sorry." He heaved a sign. "I know you're going to find it hard to believe, but I had actually planned to come clean tonight. That was my intention."

She braved a look into his eyes and saw what she hoped to be sincerity. "Come clean about what?"

"Before I tell you about my family, would you mind telling me a little about yours? Sounds strange, I know, but I've always wondered, and you never said much about them except for the fact that you miss them."

Amalie took a sip then set the mug down. In a matter of minutes, she'd told him about Mama and Papa and her brothers and sisters, about the little bayou town of Latagnier, and finally about how she ended up on a bus to Hollywood. Rob listened in silence, nodding at the appropriate moments but asking no questions.

Finally he leaned forward. "Do you remember when I told you I would go back with you when you're ready to return home?"

She nodded.

"After you hear what I have to say, if you still want me, I would like to make good on that trip to Louisiana."

A small piece of the ice coating Amalie's heart chipped and melted. Whatever he had to say, it couldn't be unforgivable. It just couldn't be.

He stepped over to the coffeepot for a refill. When he returned he captured her gaze and shook his head. "I never meant to lie to you. Honestly, except for not correcting you when you assumed Ed and I shared the same name, I was careful not to tell an outright lie."

"So your name is *not* Rob Cantoni?"

"No, not exactly. Mom wanted to call me Beau after her

great-grandfather Beauregard Crawford, the Civil War hero, but Pop won, and I got stuck with the name Roberto Antonio Lamonica Tratelli."

He paused, obviously trying to gauge her reaction. It took all her acting skills to keep the turmoil inside from showing on her face.

"The third," Rob finally added. "And, yes, my father is Roberto Tratelli Jr., the Oscar-winning director. The original Rob Tratelli—my grandfather—was a shoe salesman in Florence."

So his father made movies. The name sounded familiar, but she couldn't place it.

Not that it mattered. The fact remained that Rob had thought the worst of her.

"But why didn't you tell me?" she said on a soft breath. "Were you ashamed of me? Did you think I might not care about you if I knew? I don't understand."

Rob rose to embrace her, but she cringed and held her hands out to keep him at a distance. Defeat etching his handsome features, he returned to his chair, the blanket now in a puddle on the floor beside him.

"I didn't tell you because I thought you would be like all the others."

"Others?"

He nodded. "I know your dream of being a star, Amalie. I thought you would try to use me to get to my pop."

All the wind went out of her, and it took everything she had to ask him why.

"Look at your life, Amalie. You left everything—everyone—to come out here and be a star. If you would leave the people the Lord gave you, I reasoned you would use the ones you met here." He paused. "And that was before I knew how you'd snuck out under cover of darkness by feeding the dog your leftovers."

Time stood still as Amalie absorbed the blow his statement had dealt. Did he really believe her capable of. . .that?

"Get out!" The words flew out of Amalie's mouth before her brain registered that she had spoken.

When Rob did not move, she repeated the demand. Again he only winced. If her hands weren't shaking so bad she might have pointed to the door.

"Please, Amalie."

Rob stood and stepped over the blanket to try again to embrace her. Somehow, despite her wobbly legs, she managed to sidestep his reach without falling on her face.

"Give me a chance to explain," he said.

"A chance?" Her spine regained its starch, and she stepped forward to stab Rob's chest with her index finger. "You never gave me a chance, Rob," she said in clipped French. "You decided I was 'like the others,' whoever they are, and I would use you to get to your father." This came out in English. "*C'est tout. C'est fini.*"

"Enough? Finished? No, please, Amalie."

He'd spoken his plea in French, but the expression on his face was universal. Amalie sucked in a deep breath and held it until she saw dots swimming before her eyes. As she exhaled, she found the door and opened it.

"Go," she said. "Just go."

Rob's face paled. "I was wrong."

"Yes, well, maybe I was wrong, too."

"I didn't know you then as I know you now, Amalie. You can't fault me for making an assumption."

"Oh, can't I?" Amalie leaned against the door frame and held on tight. "I'm not sure I know you either, Rob Whoever-you-are."

That did it. Rob stormed across the room and bolted out of the door and down the hall. "And to think I actually fell in love with you!" he shouted.

"Oh, yeah? Well, to think *I* actually fell in love with *you*."

Rob froze then turned slowly to face her. "What did you say?"

Amalie's eyes narrowed. "No, what did *you* say?"

He closed the distance between them, stopping only when he reached her side. Leaning into her, he gazed into her eyes. "Do you always answer a question with a question?"

She had to remind herself to blink. "Do you?" came out in a soft whisper as their lips met.

"I'm so sorry, Amalie." Rob held tight to her. "So very sorry."

Amalie rested her head on his chest and sighed. "So am I."

"And I love you. I'm an idiot. I should have told you this, all of it, a long time ago." Abruptly Rob pulled away to hold Amalie at arm's length. "I want you to meet my parents, sweetheart. Would you do that?"

She hesitated. "Your parents? Do you really want me to?"

"You don't sound too excited about meeting them." Rob chuckled. "And to think I was afraid you would use me to get to them." He paused to cradle her cheek. "They will love you, Amalie. Don't be afraid."

"Did I say I was afraid?"

His smile lit his eyes. "You didn't have to, sweetheart. Your hands are shaking. Please don't be intimidated by who my mother and father are. You'll see when you meet them. They're just regular people."

"All right then," she said, although the idea still terrified her. "Would you also come home to Louisiana with me at Christmas to meet mine?"

"Does this mean what I think it does?"

Amalie gave him a confused look. "What?"

"Are you going home to make things right?" When she nodded weakly, he smiled. "I think it's about time, don't you?"

"I do," he said. "And speaking of 'I do,' is it too soon to ask you if you might consider me as a potential, um. . ."

Her heart thumped at the idea of what this man might

be suggesting. "Good friend?" she asked in an attempt to complete the thought.

"No, Amalie. Let me put it this way. You're the first girl I've brought home to meet my parents since the junior prom."

"And you're the first man I've brought home to meet my parents. . .ever."

"Dare I ask what that means?"

"I was wondering the same thing about your invitation."

She slipped out of his embrace to lean against the wall, arms crossed over her chest. "Oh, Rob, don't make me say it first."

"Amalie, I love you. I quite possibly may want to spend the rest of my life with you. I have pretty much known this since we met; only I let my idiotic assumptions get in the way. Do you have any idea how happy I am to know that you have no idea who my father is?"

Stunned, she could only shake her head.

"That means you love me for who I am and nothing else."

"Well, of course I do, you big goof."

"Amalie Breaux, you're an answer to prayer and the best birthday gift a guy could have." Rob let out a whoop as he lifted Amalie to twirl her in a circle. Several doors opened down the hall but closed again without complaint.

"Rob, put me down. You told me your birthday is in August."

"It is, and you're everything I wished for this year. Everything and more. Hey, I know what we'll do," he said when he set her on her feet once more. "We will spend Thanksgiving in Brentwood and Christmas in Louisiana."

"Brentwood?"

He nodded. "Yes, with my parents."

"Will Clark and Carole be there?" She giggled as his face went blank. "I'm kidding!"

"That's funny," he said as he gave her one more hug. "They usually bring the turkey." It was his turn to laugh at her expression. "Just kidding!"

sixteen

Thanksgiving Day, November 20
Brentwood, California

The last time Amalie stepped into a home this size, she'd accidentally walked into the servants' quarters on a school tour of the governor's mansion in Baton Rouge. Whereas that home held several dozen members of the governor's family and staff, Amalie knew from Rob that this one held only two: Mr. and Mrs. Roberto Tratelli Jr.

At the driveway Rob punched a buzzer, and ornate iron gates swung open on well-oiled hinges. Through the fence Amalie could see rolling acres of lush green grass that seemed to drop off into the canyon beyond. The home itself hugged the canyon wall and provided a glass and stone counterpoint to the country setting.

It was hard to believe that only a few miles down the narrow meandering road were the hustle and bustle of Hollywood and the city of Los Angeles. Why, this place was as isolated as Mama and Papa's home on the bayou.

But that was where the comparison stopped.

"Oh, Rob, I can't do this. I just can't. This is all too much."

"Don't be nervous, sweetheart. My parents will love you." Rob rolled the truck inside then stopped and turned to face her. "And, speaking of parents, have you heard from yours?"

"No, but mail moves slowly in that part of Louisiana, so they may not have the letter yet."

He cupped her cheek with his palm. "I'm glad you decided to tell them about me."

Amalie closed her eyes. The memory of writing home was still fresh, and it hadn't been easy to put her emotions on paper. Some of them, mainly remorse, defied description. For all the good that had happened in California, she now knew she should never have left home in the manner she chose.

If only Papa can forgive me.

The sound of barking dogs preceded a small band of canines, only three, though it sounded more like a half dozen. Rob climbed out of the truck and scooped up the ringleader, a black-and-white bundle of energy named Max.

While the other two, a sleek gray mixed breed and a black toy poodle, were content to perch in the bed of the truck, Max helped himself to the place between Amalie and Rob.

"My mother's band of ruffians," he said. "Pop wanted guard dogs, but Mother insisted Max and the boys could handle the job."

"I think your mother was right," Amalie said. "I doubt a car comes to the gate without being announced."

"That's the truth," he said as he scratched Max behind the ears then threw the truck into drive. Before they reached the house, Max had curled up next to Amalie and rested his fuzzy head in her lap. Rob looked over and ruffled the little guy's fur then smiled at Amalie.

"Looks like you've already passed inspection with the most difficult-to-please member of the Tratelli family."

Amalie's stomach did a flip-flop at the reminder that other Tratellis were waiting to look her over. She imagined a stern Italian man with beady eyes that missed none of her flaws and a severe blond former starlet with a penchant for running off her only son's lady loves.

Swallowing her fear, she scratched Max behind the ears then giggled when he rolled onto his back and offered her his belly. "Hey," Rob said, "looks like I've got some competition for your affection."

"Nonsense. I can love you both."

"And I love only you." Rob kissed her cheek then smoothed her hair back into place. "I do love you, Amalie Breaux. Have I mentioned that?"

She gave him a sideways glance and a broad smile. "A time or two, maybe."

"Relax." He grasped her hand and squeezed. "They're just regular people like you and me. You'll do fine."

Rob might think so, but Amalie wasn't so sure.

Before Rob could bring the truck to a halt in front of the Italian-style villa, the double doors flew open and a dark-haired man stepped out into the morning sunshine. "Welcome, welcome!" he called. "Come here, Robbie, and show me who you've brought with you."

Rob greeted his father in rapid Italian then turned to give his mother a Southern-style hug. She responded with, "Hello, honey lamb," in a voice that sounded as if she could have grown up down the bayou from Amalie.

Something about Mrs. Tratelli seemed familiar. That face, that smile. Amalie knew she'd seen her somewhere before.

And then they all turned to look at her. Three sets of eyes staring at once, two of which seemed to be waiting for the third to complete the introductions. Amalie settled her gaze on Rob, imploring him to speak. Finally he got the idea.

"Oh, sorry. Mother, Pop, this is Amalie Breaux."

Mother.

Pop.

And then she remembered why.

Amalie's fingers trembled as she reached to shake hands with the director of *Prisoner of Dreams* and then with his wife, Charlotte Crawford, the former silent film star. Her fair hair swept into a casual knot, the retired screen sensation looked every bit as beautiful as her pictures.

"Oh, Rob, she is adorable." His mother turned her blue

eyes in Amalie's direction. "I hope my son has been treating you well."

"Mother, please."

Amalie looked past the Southern beauty to exchange an amused glance with Rob. "Yes, ma'am," she said, "he's been treating me very well indeed."

Charlotte Crawford Tratelli linked arms with Amalie and led her inside. "You let me know if he steps out of line, honey lamb. I raised him to be a gentleman. Now where are you from exactly?"

The magnificence of the entry hall and the swift change of topic set her head spinning. Rob slipped up behind her to wrap his arm around her waist and steady her.

"Latagnier, Louisiana. Near New Iberia," she finally managed when she looked into Rob's eyes.

"Oh," his mother said, "a Louisiana girl. Robbie, honey, I am so proud." She turned her attention to Amalie. "You know I'm a Louisiana girl myself. My daddy worked for the railroads, and they were living in Bogalusa when I came along. I actually grew up in Charleston, but my birth certificate says Louisiana."

"Son, let me warn you about these Louisiana women." Rob's father gave his mother a quick kiss on the cheek. "Do what they ask from the beginning and save yourself the trouble of arguing. You're going to give in anyway."

"Yes, sir, Pop." Rob leaned in to whisper in Amalie's ear. "See, I told you they would love you."

"Well, of course we do," Mrs. Tratelli said. "The question is, since you obviously love her, what do you intend to do about it, Rob?"

"Mother!"

His mother put on an innocent look while his father chuckled. "See what I mean, son?"

"Lunch is ready," Cook called from the doorway.

"Good," Rob said. "I was beginning to think I was the only thing roasting."

"Oh, is it warm in here, darling?" his mother asked as Mr. Tratelli led her into the dining room.

"Only when you start asking questions, Mother." He entwined his fingers with Amalie's and followed them. "Looks like Cook has outdone herself."

"Honey, Cook didn't make all this. I did." His mother turned her attention to Amalie. "Cooking is a hobby of mine. The truth be known, I have recipes I couldn't possibly turn over to anyone who wasn't a family member."

"Really?"

Mrs. Tratelli touched her arm. "That's right, honey lamb, but I have a feeling you'll get hold of Granny Kate's turkey recipe before long." She gestured in Rob's direction. "He's crazy about you, Amalie. Did you know that?"

"I, well, um. . .yes."

"And I suspect you told him you love him, too."

Amalie nodded.

Rob's mother leaned toward her so that anyone watching would think they were talking girl-talk. "Did he tell you about us before or after you fell in love with him?"

Amalie looked Mrs. Tratelli in the eye as she straightened her spine and squared her shoulders. "After, ma'am," she said. "While this is all very nice, I love Rob for the man I met cooking burgers at the diner."

The tone in Mrs. Tratelli's voice and the expression on her face left nothing to the imagination. This was a mother whose primary interest was in protecting her son.

"And what if I told you that, upon our death, everything Roberto and I have is going to the missions we support? That as much as we love our son, he won't inherit a dime from us?"

The answer to that question was easy. "Mrs. Tratelli, I grew up with nothing. One of ten kids in a house with three bedrooms and a privy out back. But we were happy, and we loved the Lord. My mama taught me that some of the most unhappy people around were the ones with too much money and not enough faith."

Amalie paused to try to gauge whether she'd spoken too plainly. The knowing look on Mrs. Tratelli's face told her she could continue.

"So to answer your question, ma'am," Amalie said, "I would have to say praise God that so many people will benefit from the blessings the Lord has bestowed on you and Mr. Tratelli. As for Rob and me, I believe we'd be happy as can be wherever the Lord sends us."

Mrs. Tratelli stared intently back at Amalie then began to smile. "Yes, indeed," she said as she grasped Amalie's hand and squeezed it, "I do believe you and I are going to get along just fine."

"What are you two plotting?" the elder Tratelli called. "Dare I ask?"

Winking at Amalie, Mrs. Tratelli shook her head. "Nothing you two need to know about. Just girl-talk about menfolk, isn't that right, honey?"

"What say we eat before Mother gives away all the family secrets?" Rob said.

"Excellent idea," his father said. "I am anxious to get to know your Amalie better. Come, and we will give our heavenly Father thanks before partaking of the Thanksgiving meal."

Amalie discovered that, rather than pray seated, the Tratellis held hands and said their blessing over the meal while standing. Being invited into the circle, Amalie listened while Rob's father gave an eloquent prayer.

"And many blessings this day, Father, for the family who is missing their daughter Amalie. Their loss on this day is our family's great gain."

Four amens later and the prayer was finished, but the Italian patriarch's words settled in her heart.

The family who is missing their daughter.

A lump formed in Amalie's throat, but she forced a smile. Until this moment she had never admitted to herself how very much she missed home. She had also never considered that those at home might be missing her.

At once Christmas seemed too far away.

The talk during lunch in the elegant dining room overlooking the pool turned to the war and then to Congress. Finally the three Tratellis took up a lively discussion of the motion picture industry in general and the father's new movie in particular.

Through it all, Amalie found her attention focused more on her companion than on the topic. While her initial star-struck feeling had all but disappeared, the feeling that she somehow did not belong here lingered.

Until Rob reached under the table to take her hand. Then he gave her a sideways glance and added a grin.

And suddenly she was home.

seventeen

Rob put the truck in PARK at the edge of the Pacific Coast overlook then shut off the engine. Instantly the rhythmic sound of crashing waves and the screech of gulls filled the truck. So did the salty wet smell of the Pacific Ocean.

Never had he taken anyone to his favorite thinking spot; trips here were usually reserved for times to meet with his Savior. Today, however, his heart swelled with love for Amalie Breaux, and his mind was torn with the news he had to give her.

Not the state in which he had expected to find himself when he planned this evening.

When he pledged his love, he'd promised himself that Amalie's dreams would become his dreams, too. He figured prayer would take care of that messy gray area where the possibility of Amalie becoming a movie star lurked.

Rob's dilemma was clear. He wanted her happy but feared what would most make her happy. And so far the Lord hadn't breathed a word of His plans other than a single statement: *Perfect love casts out fear.*

Perfect love. Rob sighed. *If only I weren't so imperfect.*

He searched his mind for another line of thinking—anything to return his spirits to the heights they had soared while seated next to Amalie at dinner. Amalie seemed content, though, to sit beside him staring at the waves and resting her head on his shoulder. His ladylove, it seemed, was the picture of contentment.

"So," he finally said, "what did you think of my parents?"

She lifted her head to look into his eyes. Her smile dawned

bright and genuine. "Oh, Rob, they were wonderful. Not at all what I expected." At his confused look Amalie clarified. "Oh, that didn't sound right. What I mean is, they were just as you said—*normal.*"

"And what did you expect?" Rob wrapped his arm around her waist and scooted her closer. "Something out of a movie, perhaps? Maybe a scene from *The Philadelphia Story*?"

"Very funny." She paused. "It's just that everyone in California is so different from bayou people," Amalie finally said. "I guess I thought they would be, oh, I don't know, stuffy."

"Stuffy?" Rob chuckled. "Now that you've met Mother, can you imagine anyone less stuffy?"

"There's just one thing." She snuggled into his shoulder. "When you meet my family. . ."

"Yes?" he whispered against the top of her head.

"Let's just say it won't be quite as formal."

"I expect it won't," he said with a chuckle. "Something wrong with that?"

"Oh, no, but. . ."

"But?"

She shrugged. "But there are so many of them, my family, that is. And someone is always talking over someone else, and there's usually a baby or two making a ruckus. Then there're my brothers. They seem to think teasing is an appropriate topic for dinner conversation. Oh, and my papa—let's just say he can be the strong silent type, until he has something to say. Then you never know what will come out of his mouth. And Mama, oh, can she cook! But as far as the formal meal, she's most happy when we're passing the plates and dipping gumbo out of the pot in the middle of the table."

Rob leaned back against the door and turned Amalie to face him. "Sweetheart, replace that pot of gumbo with a big batch of spaghetti and meatballs and you've got the average Tratelli meal."

She looked skeptical.

"See, you may have noticed my father is Italian." When she grinned, he continued. "Long before war threatened in Italy, Pop started finding jobs for his family over here. Gradually he convinced all of his siblings and much of his extended family to take him up on his offer to settle here in California."

"Really?"

Rob nodded. "You've already met Ed and Uncle Gio."

"Yes."

"Well, let's just say if all my relatives got together, which they do at least once a month, there would be no use for the word *formal*." He smiled. "In fact, did you happen to notice that pair of long tables set under the trees past the pool?"

"Yes, I wondered what those were for."

"Family gatherings," he said. "Italians love to make a meal dramatic. Pop and his merry band spend hours at the tables while the women and children overrun the house and grounds. It's a sight to see."

"I would like very much to see it." A frown turned her soft lips downward as her gaze tilted to meet his. "Rob?"

"Yes?"

"Why didn't they invite the family to meet me? After all, it was Thanksgiving. Maybe they didn't expect to like me."

Rob gathered her into his arms once more. "Oh, no, sweetheart, that's not it at all." He kissed the top of her head. "They were afraid it would be too much for you. Mother elected to initiate you into the family gradually rather than all at once. Wait until New Year's Eve. You'll meet all of them, and I have to warn you."

"What?"

"They will all love you, which will be a blessing and a curse. Once you join an Italian family, you're in it for life. If you try to leave, they follow you."

"Oh, stop it, Rob," she said as she settled back against his shoulder. "Besides, why would I ever want to leave?"

How long they sat watching the waves dance in the winter sun, Rob couldn't say. When he worked up the courage to broach the next subject, the sun had worked its way across the sky to tease the horizon. Already a few overachieving stars had begun to pulse bright white in the purple dusk. Soon there would be thousands.

"Sweetheart," he said softly, "you know I love you."

"And I love you," she answered.

"I want you to know some things."

Her silence surprised him. Finally she grasped his hand. "What is it?"

"I need to tell you about my cousin Helena and what Hollywood did to her." He related the story of his childhood companion's rise and fall in sparse terms. To add detail would be too hard. Amalie need not know more than this: A career in the movies could be a woman's fondest dream and her worst nightmare.

"Oh, Rob, I'm so sorry," she said as tears shimmered in her eyes. "Now I see why you didn't care for my ambitions."

Here it is. My big opportunity. Do I tell her that no wife of mine will be an actress, or do I support her dreams and pray they somehow fit with mine?

Rob considered his words carefully, mindful of the way he'd hoped the evening would go. As he opened his mouth to speak, a still small voice whispered in his ear, *Perfect love casts out fear.*

"Amalie," he said, "I was wrong. I shouldn't have assumed that what happened to Helena would someday happen to you, too. Would you forgive me for all the times I turned my fear into a bad temper?"

Amalie's tears spilled in earnest, and Rob wiped them with his handkerchief. Had he said the wrong thing?

"Oh, Rob, there's nothing to forgive. You were trying to

keep me safe, and I understand that now." She nestled against him. "I've wondered lately if the Lord allowed me to come here to act or to meet you."

Stunned, Rob could only hold her tight. He'd never thought of that. Maybe the Lord didn't intend Amalie to make her living on a Hollywood sound stage. Maybe. . .

Perfect love casts out fear.

"Sweetheart?"

"Yes?"

Outside more stars joined the brave adventurers until the deep purple depths of the sky wore a sprinkling of diamonds. It would be a lovely evening. Too bad things were not going as planned.

"I've been wondering about something." *Courage. Lord, give me courage.*

"What's that, Rob?"

"What did Tillie say to you at the diner that day you met her?" *I know I'm a coward, Lord. But the next topic will be the one I believe You want me to tackle.*

Amalie chuckled. "Why?"

Because I'm stalling for time. "Just curious. As I recall, it put a smile on your face for the rest of the day."

Amalie shifted positions but did not look up into his eyes. Instead she sighed. "If you must know, she told me she believed God had promised her that if she found somewhere to go for a few months, you would come to work at the diner and a young lady would show up and steal your heart."

"Is that right?" He paused. "How about that?"

Amalie nodded. "Yes, how about that?"

"She was right," he said softly. "A certain young lady did show up—and she has stolen my heart."

And my dreams.

The thought startled him. With the negotiations nearly complete, Rob and Uncle Gio were very close to having the delivery company they'd planned for and prayed about. Only a week or two stood between them and the accomplishment of their dreams.

By the first week in January, Rob could take his place as president of Star Aviation with Uncle Gio as CEO. After that, the sky was the limit, literally and figuratively.

But what would become of this dream if his lovely Amalie wasn't by his side? He knew from his pop that making movies was not all sound stage and signing autographs. There were months, sometimes years, of hard work, often at far-flung locations.

Would his wife be content to spend her days there without him? Worse, if her career took off, what were the odds she would want to end it in favor of a family? Where would his dreams of a quiet, simple life be? Would his children endure the glare of fame as Rob had?

Lord, if this is meant to be, I know You will work it out—of that I have no doubt. What I don't understand is how. It's one thing to say that hunger is bad, and it's another to have a growling belly.

"Actually I have some good news for you. I was contemplating how to pass it along."

"Oh?"

He nodded. "Remember when Mother took you out to look at her garden?"

"Yes."

"Well, Pop and I had an interesting discussion while you were gone."

"Really?" She smiled. "Anything you can tell me about?"

Another moment of truth. Everything in him wanted to say no.

Perfect love.

Rob took a deep breath and let it out slowly. The sun had set, and the shadows hid his expression. While he might be able to manage a confession, he knew he probably would not be as successful at masking his expression of doubt.

He might be selfish enough to want her with him rather than out making movies, but at least he knew that about himself. What he also knew was that Amalie Breaux would lay down her career for him if he asked; she was that sort of woman.

The engagement ring in his pocket, the one he'd hoped to give her tonight at the beach, would have to stay there, at least for now. Amalie had a dream, and he would not be the reason she did not see it fulfilled.

"Actually it is," he said slowly. "Pop wants you to try for a spot in his next movie."

eighteen

Amalie lay in bed that night, unable to keep her thoughts from pushing away sleep. What a day. It was too much to take in. Too much to consider.

In the blink of an eye she'd gone from a simple bayou girl in love with a fry cook to an actress about to audition for the man who could someday become her father-in-law. "*Le bon Dieu mait la main*," she whispered. "Help me, Father."

Amalie rose and settled in the chair, wrapping the quilt around her to ward off the night's chill. A letter tucked into her Bible beckoned, and she reached for it. She recognized Papa's scrawl. He must have written as soon as her letter reached them.

The letter came yesterday, delivered to the apartment across the hall by mistake and slid beneath her door this morning with a note. She'd slipped both into her Bible thinking to read the letter after her Thanksgiving meal with the Tratellis. Her frantic state left her unable to consider reading what Papa might have to say beforehand.

She tore it open carefully and smiled at the greeting. "*Bonjour, jeune fille. C'est Papa*" was written in broad strokes with a fountain pen on formal writing paper.

"Well, of course, it is you, Papa," she whispered. "And since when do you refer to me as 'young lady'?"

"*Gete toi*," she read next. *Watch out for yourself.* "That's my papa."

He went on to write about the weather, the family, and finally his fishing and trapping success over the past months. At the end of the first page his chatty tone turned more somber. "This man you mention, he is a good man, yes?"

"Yes, Papa," Amalie whispered. "He is a very good man. You would like him."

"These feelings you profess for him, they are sudden," he wrote. "But in these uncertain times with men devouring freedom like so much white rice and gumbo over in Europe, who am I to say what is too fast? Perhaps *le bon Dieu*, He has sent you far from me to find that man."

Amalie held the letter to her chest and smiled. "I hope so, Papa," she said as she gathered the papers and turned once more to her reading.

Somewhere in the middle of page two, he must have stopped writing temporarily, for when the next paragraph began he had taken up his pencil. A smudge of ink in the shape of a partial fingerprint stained the edge of the page, and Amalie pressed her forefinger against it before reading further.

"Ma conscience me fait mal, Amalie." My conscience hurts.

The page began to swim in her hands, and Amalie set it aside to wipe her tears with the corner of her quilt. "Oh, Papa," she whispered as she reached for the crisp white paper once more.

"Il n'a in bon boute." It's been a good while. *"S'il vous plaît rentrer."* Please come home. *"Je t'aime."* I love you. *"Dieu te beni."* God bless you. He signed it, *Your Stubborn Papa*.

Amalie sat for a long time staring at the envelope, the folded pages, and the ink-smudged fingerprint. Home. Family. Mama and Papa. Her heart hurt for those things, and yet she couldn't leave.

Not until she followed this opportunity to see where it would lead.

Amalie made her way over to the desk and pulled out a sheet of stationery, settling into the little chair with the quilt still wrapped around her. Words swam before her eyes, and she had to stop more than once. Finally she had the first few words down on paper, words of a general nature that spoke of how much she missed what she'd left behind.

"I will return to Latagnier someday soon, Papa. I promise," she said as she translated the thought to Papa's native Acadian and printed it on the page. "*Je me retournerai à Latagnier un jour bientôt, Papa. Je promets.*" Somehow the promise seemed much more concrete when written in the language of her youth.

She went on to write about Rob and the Thanksgiving dinner she shared with his parents, carefully leaving out their connection to the film industry. Pen poised over the page, she considered how best to tell them of her upcoming December 1 audition for a film called *Lady Sleuth*.

When nothing came, she set the pen down. "Tomorrow, after I've slept," she said as she and the quilt headed for bed. "Or maybe the next day."

Two days later she managed a reply, leaving the conflicting emotions she felt out of the words she wrote. Promising to tell Papa all about her adventures in Hollywood in person, she informed him she would be coming home for a visit at Christmas and bringing Rob.

"*Sa va bien, Papa.*" Things are going well. "*C'est pas de ta faute.*" I don't blame you.

What else?

Amalie stared at the words, all of them true. Facing Papa would be even more difficult than responding to his letter, but she would manage both.

❧

Friday, November 28

Amalie arrived at the diner a full half-hour early for the lunch shift and found Ed hard at work on a faucet in the kitchen. "I thought you were the owner now," she called as she put on her apron and name tag.

Ed gave the wrench another turn then swiped at his brow. "Precisely why I am doing this job myself," he said. "Do I let any man off the street who claims he is a plumber touch my sink? No." And with that he ducked under the sink.

"What's that banging noise?"

Amalie whirled to see Rob standing a few feet away. "I didn't hear you come in."

"I wonder why!" Rob shouted.

Amalie grinned. "Ed's doing some plumbing work." She pointed to the kitchen. "Seems as though he's particular about who touches things now that he owns the place."

Rob gestured to the door. "Let's talk outside."

She donned her sweater to follow him to the sidewalk. When Rob settled on the bench at the corner bus stop, she sat beside him. "What's up?"

"A couple of things actually," he said. "First, I want to show you something." He pulled an envelope out of his jacket pocket. "It's the contract."

"For the office space at the airport?"

Rob nodded. "All I have to do is sign it, and it's mine. Well," he amended, "mine and Uncle Gio's."

"Oh, Rob, that's so exciting.

"It is," he said, "but I'm not going to rush into this. I think the project needs a little more prayer. Could we do that—together?"

"Right now? Of course."

"Now and until I feel the Lord has given me the go-ahead," he said.

After they prayed, Rob gathered Amalie into his arms and kissed her hair. "Thank you. I feel good knowing you're praying with me. I want this to be for both of us. And," he said slowly, "for our children."

Amalie's heart soared at the near-proposal. If only the man would come right out and say what she had been thinking and he had been hinting. They were meant for each other and for marriage.

Somehow she maintained a cool façade as she offered nothing more than a smile and a nod of her head. An eternity and three city buses went by before Rob spoke again.

"That's not the only reason I dropped by today, Amalie," Rob said. "I have something else for you."

Any effort to hide her excitement must have failed, for Rob's surprised look was obvious. "Well, I hope this lives up to your expectation." He reached into his pocket and retrieved a folded slip of paper. "Ah, here it is."

Interesting. Did he intend to read his proposal? *Well, no matter. As long as he gets to the "will you" part so I can get to the "yes, I will." That's all that matters.*

Rather than read the document, he thrust the paper in her direction. "Pop sent this."

What? She unfolded the paper to find an Imperial Studios gate pass dated December 1, 1941.

"That's for your audition," Rob said. "Monday at ten o'clock. See?" He pointed to the information regarding the location of the set and the name of the casting director. "Pop said it's only a formality. He wants you for the film but has to have some audition footage to placate the investors."

She looked up, speechless. In her hand she held the key to her childhood dreams, the answer to prayers she'd sent heavenward for as long as she could remember.

And yet at that moment she would have given it to the next person who walked past the bus stop in exchange for a marriage proposal from Rob Tratelli.

The realization of that fact stunned her. Rob must have taken her silence for happiness, for he gave her a hug and a smile.

"I'm happy, too, Amalie," he said. "Really I am. It looks like our fondest dreams are coming true."

"Yes, they are, aren't they?"

She put on a broad smile. Funny how those things she thought she always wanted paled in comparison to what she knew she needed.

She almost handed the paper back to him. Almost, but not quite.

Something in her said to give it a try. If she didn't, she might not know what she'd missed.

Or, worse, she might miss something better than being Mrs. Rob Tratelli. Thoughts of what she might miss took hold until she became excited over the prospect of a film career and a family.

Surely it could be done. Rob's mother certainly managed. Look how wonderful he turned out. Why couldn't she have her dream and Rob?

"Go with me, Rob." The words were out before she realized she'd said them. "Please," she added. "I don't want to go alone."

"I, um, well. . ." He looked away. "I don't think I can do that, sweetheart."

Amalie grasped his hand and squeezed. "Why not?"

Rob swung his gaze to meet hers. For a moment she thought he might speak. Instead he shook his head.

"All right then," she said slowly. "It'll be fine. I can manage."

He seemed doubtful. "Are you sure, Amalie?"

She nodded. "Of course I am. Now I'd better get back inside before my boss fires me."

Rob affected a fierce look. "He'd better not fire you, or he will have me to answer to."

Amalie giggled. "As terrifying as you look, you don't need to defend me. If I get the part I'll have to quit anyway."

Rob grew silent and seemed to be more interested in the Wilshire-bound bus at the curb than in her. She gave his hand another squeeze, and he responded with a weak smile.

"Dreams coming true, remember?" she said as she leaned her head on his shoulder.

"Yeah," he responded, "dreams coming true. Isn't it great?"

nineteen

Amalie checked her reflection in the mirror one more time before reaching for her purse. Too little sleep and too many jangled nerves showed in her eyes.

"That's what stage makeup is for," she said. "To hide all your flaws and troubles." But stage makeup couldn't hide the trouble grieving her heart.

Since Friday she'd been trying to pray about her audition— only to find she had no idea what to pray. Yesterday Reverend Kendall's sermon had been on listening to the Lord and heeding His call.

Usually the pastor's words left her with thoughts to meditate on and actions to follow. This time, however, she felt confused.

How do you listen to the Lord when He seems to offer only silence?

Amalie reached for the knob as the bell rang. She opened the door to find Rob standing there.

"Your car is here, Miss Breaux," he said with a sweeping bow. "Truck, that is. I hope you don't mind, but Pop's Rolls was being washed."

"You're kidding, right?" she said with a giggle.

Rob reached behind her to close the apartment door then checked to be sure it locked properly. When he linked arms with her, his grin broadened.

"Kidding? Oh, no, I'm quite serious. The car was filthy. You should have seen it. But you, now. . ." Rob held her at arm's length and turned her in a circle. "You look like a movie star." His grin softened. "Really, honey, you do."

"Thank you," she said softly. "Do you tell that to all the others?"

"Amalie, sweetheart," he said softly as he gathered her into an embrace, "there are no others. You're all I want and all I need." After a quick kiss he added, "And a whole lot more than I ever dreamed God would bless me with."

"Oh, Rob," she said softly. "I—"

He touched his finger to her lips, stilling the voice that longed to tell him she felt the same.

At the curb, Rob helped Amalie into the truck then closed the door and hurried around to climb in the driver's side. The few miles to Imperial Studios were spent in silence. Amalie tried once more to pray against the fears that were threatening her.

Perfect love casts out fear.

Amalie cast a sideways glance at Rob, half-hoping he might have heard the same thing. His attention turned to the road ahead, Rob seemed oblivious that God had spoken to her.

Closing her eyes, Amalie formulated a response. *Yes, Father, but I'm far from perfect.*

To her surprise, she received an immediate response. *But I am.*

"You're awfully quiet, Amalie."

She smiled. "Just having a little conversation with the Lord."

Rob nodded. "I've been doing a lot of that myself this morning."

When he failed to elaborate, she let the subject drop. Up ahead the twin gold crowns on the black iron gates of Imperial Studios loomed. Rather than drive toward the guardhouse, Rob turned the truck into a parking spot across the street.

"This is as far as I go, sweetheart," he said as he turned to face her. "It's important to me that you do this on your own."

She nodded and managed a weak "Of course." When her voice allowed, she added, "I wouldn't have it any other way."

"Can I pray for you right now? For us?"

"Sure," she said as she scooted into his embrace.

"Father, only You know what is best for Amalie and me. See to it that we do Your will, even if it means giving up our right to what we think we want. Be a beacon and a guiding light so we can more easily follow You. I'm sending Amalie forth with a talent that only You could have given her. Let Your will be done inside those studio gates, and if You intend her to act in the movies, let Your light shine through her. Most of all, God, don't let her be afraid. Keep her always mindful that perfect love casts out fear."

☙

"And one more thing, Father," Rob whispered as he watched the love of his life cross the street and show her pass to the guard. "Please bring her back to me. I don't care how You do it or how long it takes—just bring her back."

She disappeared inside in a swirl of blue skirts, and his hopes and dreams went with her. Soon she'd be showered with attention, first from wardrobe then makeup. Then she would practice her lines and shoot her test.

Rob sighed. He should have insisted she forget this nonsense and marry him at once. After she'd had a taste of the entertainment world, she might find she liked it a lot better than settling down to be a pilot's wife.

If only he'd insisted. After all, the ugly side of Hollywood was hard to see when the spotlights shone in your eyes.

Pop told him Amalie might spend the rest of the day at the studios, especially if the screen test yielded a favorable response from the staff. He even offered to send his car to wait for Amalie and bring her home afterward. As much as

Rob knew Amalie would get a kick out of riding around in the Rolls, he had declined Pop's offer.

Now he wondered if he'd made a mistake.

Maybe he ought to head home and let Pop know he'd changed his mind. If Amalie chose the stage over the nursery, why not send her out of his life in style?

Throwing the truck into reverse, he gave it some gas and spun out of the parking spot. A few minutes later he headed for the cliff overlooking the beach and his favorite thinking spot.

❧

Amalie held tight to the edge of the golf cart's cold plastic seat as her guide turned a corner on two wheels, barely missing a sign that read "Studio A."

"Here we are," the fellow called as the cart rolled to an abrupt stop in a parking space reserved for the director. "Nice to meet ya, Miss Bow. Break a leg!"

"That's Breaux," she said as her heels touched solid ground. His response was a quick wave as the cart dashed around the corner and disappeared from sight.

Wouldn't she know it? She'd finally managed to get inside the gates of a studio only to end up alone. "It sure would be nice to run into Mignon Dupree or Stu Stevens about now," she said to no one.

"Good luck, sweetheart. Last I heard both of them were unemployed."

She turned to follow the sound of the rough voice. "Mr. Bogart?"

The star tipped his fedora and disappeared into the door marked Stage 1A. To the right of that door was another marked Stage 1B. The only thing that distinguished A from B was the flashing red light atop B.

Amalie stood there for a full minute before she decided which door to enter. If she had indeed seen Humphrey Bogart, the one with the red flashing light looked like a good choice, so she strolled over to open it.

"Cut!" someone yelled. "Who opened the door?"

A moment later Amalie was sent scurrying down the hall with an aide and a scolding. "I'm terribly sorry," she told the aide. "I had no idea the flashing light meant they were filming."

"In here, Miss Bow." The aide pointed to a brightly lit room with racks of clothing on either side. "This is the wardrobe department. Ruby will be with you shortly."

"It's Breaux," she said as the door shut. A garish red dress with a matching fur-lined cape hung from a peg behind the door. A red hat with a long black feather completed the outfit.

"If that's what I'm supposed to wear, I might as well go home now."

Amalie reached for the tag and gasped when she read the name on it. Several other tags yielded equally impressive celebrity names. Finally her hands found a purple velvet cloak and gown and pulled it from the rack. She didn't have to read the tag to know it belonged to Mignon Dupree.

She'd seen it on the movie screen in the closing scene of *Prisoner of Dreams*. The scene where Mignon's character recovered all she'd lost and everything ended as it should.

Then it hit her. She, Amalie Breaux, from Latagnier, Louisiana, was standing in the wardrobe room of Imperial Studios.

Had it been only a few months ago she'd climbed out the window of her parents' home to meet the bus in New Iberia?

"Miss Bow, would you come with me, please? The casting director is ready for you."

"That's Breaux, and are you sure? What happened to wardrobe?" She turned to see a man in a dark suit disappear into the hall. Following him, she ended up in another small, windowless room.

"Sit there." He pointed toward a table situated in the corner. "He'll be with you momentarily."

"He?"

Amalie jumped as the door shut then jumped again when it opened. A small man with a thick shock of unruly dark hair bounded into the room and tossed a sheaf of papers on the table.

"Sign here. And don't forget to initial the bottom of each page."

"What is it?"

Once again he motioned toward the table. "Your contract, Miss Bow. You'll need to sign it in order for it to take effect."

She crossed the distance to the table and peered down at the document. "But this is a contract."

The little man let out a sigh. "Yes, that's what I said. What were you expecting?"

Amalie looked up at him. "An audition."

The room echoed with the man's laughter. "You are funny," he said. "No wonder Mr. Tratelli suggested you to play the part of Diandra. You're perfect for it."

"Diandra?" She shook her head. "I don't know what you're talking about, sir. I was told I would be doing an audition today with a screen test."

"Oh, that's rich." The fellow shrugged. "I suppose I could order a screen test, but my instructions were to bring you a contract and wait while you sign it."

"But that means. . ."

"You got the part," he supplied. "Yeah, big surprise, right?"

twenty

Rob slumped against the steering wheel, defeated. Five minutes in his favorite spot, and his brain shut down completely. Prayer came in fits and starts until he decided he might as well pray while he drove.

It all came down to one issue. Either Amalie wanted to be his wife, or she wanted to be a star. While he knew he would take her either way, he had a strong suspicion she might feel differently.

A few years in the business and she might not look at home and family the same. Worse, he thought, she might not look at him the same either. And even if all those things fell into line and she managed to love him and her movie career, what would happen to their children? Of all the things he'd learned as the son of movie people, the most important was how to live his life in a fishbowl.

He never wanted that for his sons and daughters.

Given the fact that Amalie had been waiting for her big break most of her life, the odds were not in his favor that she might choose to walk away now. Still, he knew he had to find that out for himself.

All the way back to Imperial Studios he'd asked himself why he bothered to hope things might go his way, and each time the answer was the same. *Because I love her.*

He turned off the radio and its incessant predictions of battles won and lost. Sure, the atrocities of war and the threat to freedom would probably draw the Americans in sooner rather than later, but all the debate in the world wasn't going to change the outcome.

Only the Lord could do that.

Opening the glove compartment, he parted the jumble of maps and spare pieces of paper to find the small black box. A flash of blue caught his attention, and he looked up in time to see Amalie crossing the street.

"That was fast." Rob slammed the glove compartment shut then climbed out of the truck and stood beside it as she approached.

"Oh, Rob," she said, "I'm so glad you're still here."

"Where else would I be, sweetheart?" he asked as she ran into his embrace.

Amalie held on tightly to Rob until he pulled back and held her at arm's length. She was shaking.

"All right now—tell me what happened."

"Oh, Rob, it is such a big place. I mean, I never dreamed that many people worked inside a studio." She paused to give him a sheepish look. "And I learned what a flashing red light means outside a studio door. I also found out what happens when you open the door and the light is flashing."

Rob cringed. "It wasn't pleasant, I'm assuming."

"Not at all," she said. "I mean, the people were nice enough. Oh, and I saw Humphrey Bogart." She shook her head. "He wasn't as tall as I expected, and he called me sweetheart."

"Sounds like him."

"You mean you know Humphrey Bogart?" She sighed. "Oh, never mind. Of course you would know Humphrey Bogart."

"We've met."

He didn't mention that Pop played tennis with the man every Monday morning or that he generally showed up at Casa Tratelli whenever he was in need of a dose of Mother's Southern cooking, especially her buttermilk cornbread. He'd tried for years to garner the secret recipe Mother inherited from Nana Miller.

Rob chuckled. The odds were Mr. Bogart had just come

from beating the socks off Pop and then buying him coffee.

"Why am I not surprised?" she said. "I keep forgetting this is normal for you."

All he could do was shrug. She would soon learn that people were people, even though some managed to have their faces on the movie screen while others picked up trash, drove a bus, or flew an airplane. A job was a job.

That was one of the positive things about being a Hollywood kid. It gave you an interesting perspective on people and fame.

And growing up a Christian Hollywood kid added another dimension to the picture. Rob had discovered, to his dismay, that some of the brightest lights in the business were the most miserable. He gave thanks every day that Mother and Pop raised him to love the Lord more than anything or anyone else.

Having Jesus to answer to helped put everything else in perspective. That was one of the things from his youth that he intended to pass on to his children.

"So you *did* get your interview with the casting director, right?" He checked his watch. She'd been inside the Imperial gates less than an hour. Thirty-eight minutes to be exact.

"Oh, yes, I finally managed to see him, after they had me wait awhile in the wardrobe room. There was one thing, though."

He touched her chin with his forefinger and smiled. Oh, but she was adorable. "What was that, sweetheart?"

"Wherever I went, everyone called me Miss Bow." Amalie gestured toward her dark hair and eyes. "It was maddening. Do I look as if I could be related to Clara Bow?"

"You look like a little slice of heaven right here on earth, Amalie. I'm just glad it's all over." He looked past her to the gates of Imperial Studios then returned his attention to Amalie. "Did they tell you when the decision would be made? I assume someone will have to look over the screen test first.

That's usually how it happens."

"There was no screen test," she said. "And the decision seems to have been made before I ever showed up."

"Oh, sweetheart, I'm so sorry. I know you were counting on this, and I thought you would have the part."

Amalie looked up into his eyes, barely blinking. "That's just it, Rob—I *did* get the part."

"Oh." He leaned against the truck for support. Of course. Pop would make sure she had no competition. Thanks to his connections, Amalie Breaux would be a star. "That's great, honey," he managed. "When do you start?"

She smiled. "I don't. I told them thanks but no thanks."

Rob shook his head. Had he really heard what he thought he'd heard? "Honey, I'm going to need more information than that."

She surprised him by slipping past him to climb into the truck. "I intend to tell you all about it, but could we go somewhere besides here?" By the time he had the engine running, she settled on a spot. "Would you take me to your thinking place?"

"The beach?"

"That's right. I want to feel the sand under my feet and run around in the waves like a mad woman." She touched his sleeve. "I grew up next to a bayou where I was in the water all the time, but I've never been swimming in the ocean."

"Amalie, it's the first day of December."

"I noticed," she said.

"All right then, the beach it is, but we stay in the truck. I promise to take you swimming in the Pacific as soon as it warms up around here."

"We'll see," she said.

"Yes," he responded. "We *will* see."

The ten-minute drive took forever. Rob kept casting sideways glances at his passenger to be sure she was still smiling.

Each time he peeked in her direction, her grin had broadened. By the time he shut off the engine, she could have been posing for a toothpaste commercial.

"It's a glorious day, Rob—don't you think?"

"It is." He hadn't taken his eyes off her since the engine stopped, so it could have been raining cats and dogs with bolts of lightning streaking across the sky for all he knew. "Definitely glorious."

She began to scoot toward him then seemed to think better of it. "Can we take a walk?"

"A walk?" Rob glanced down at her dress and new patent leather pumps. "You're hardly wearing beach clothes, honey, and it's chilly out. I thought we decided to wait until it got warmer."

"You decided." Amalie shrugged. "Me, I don't care a bit. I just can't sit here any longer." She bolted from the truck then shed her shoes and tossed them in the back. "Oh, Rob, this feels glorious."

"Glorious," he repeated. "That seems to be the theme of the day."

Rob sat and watched a moment before realizing she meant to make good on her threat. Then he might as well make good on something, too. He opened the glove compartment and took out the object he'd carried around far too long and stuck it in his pocket.

"Slow down, Amalie," he called, knowing full well she would ignore him.

Picking his way down the rock-strewn path to the shore in bare feet was less than glorious, as was the feel of icy waves on his skin. For Amalie, it seemed as though she'd been transported elsewhere, to a place much warmer than this.

"Where are you going?" he called as he rolled up the legs of his trousers.

"Anywhere." She began to run, dodging waves and stomping

in their wake. Her skirts circled and swirled, and her hair glistened a deep blue black.

"You're going to catch your death of cold if you don't stop that."

"No, I won't!" she shouted. "But if I did, at least I know where I'm going." She chased a gull until it flew away. "Are you coming, or are you just going to watch?"

"For now I'm enjoying watching."

"All right, you old fuddy-duddy."

He watched the love of his life play like the children he hoped they would have, and the only word he could think of was, "Glorious."

ая

The telephone rang poolside at Casa Tratelli, and Charlotte answered. She'd been interrupted in the middle of a particularly interesting part of her study of the book of Daniel, but she tried not to let her irritation show. After all, few knew this number, so it must be important.

She recognized the caller's voice immediately. "Darling, it's the studio," she called.

Roberto set down his paintbrush and stepped away from the watercolor he'd been working on since Humphrey left. They exchanged a glance before he took the phone.

"Tratelli here," he said. "How did it go?"

As the conversation on the other end of the phone continued, Charlotte watched her husband's face. A marriage of nearly thirty years taught a woman that the expression on a man's face often told more of the story than what came out of his mouth. At this moment Roberto wore surprise, but as he hung up the phone she saw contentment set in.

"Well?" she said. "What happened?"

He reached for her hand and led her to the painting. "You were right, dear," he said as he kissed her soundly. "You were absolutely right about our Amalie."

Our Amalie. Charlotte smiled and then rested her head on Roberto's shoulder. *Thank You, Lord.*

"Honey lamb, I believe we need to build a gazebo," she said.

She felt Roberto chuckle. "And what use would this gazebo have, my love? Surely you do not intend to house the missionaries there as well?"

"Oh, no," Charlotte said as she entwined her fingers with her husband's. "But wouldn't it be a splendid place for a springtime wedding?"

"And if the bride wishes to speak her vows elsewhere, say among her people in Louisiana—then what?"

Charlotte peered up at the man she loved, a man whose exterior had aged a bit but whose heart remained the same as the day they met. "All the better, Roberto," she said with a grin. "A Southern wedding is perfect."

Roberto smiled then kissed the tip of her nose. "Ah, and I am a man who can appreciate perfection when I see it."

twenty-one

Over the sound of the wind and the waves Rob called Amalie's name.

"Come here," he said. "I'm freezing, and I need to ask you something."

She giggled and ran faster. "Catch me if you can," she called.

He did. After he'd kissed her soundly, he dropped to one knee right there in the cold wet sand. *Amalie, vous m'épouserez?*

"Marry you? Oh, Rob."

He waited an eternity for her to speak. Finally he asked, " 'Oh, Rob,' what?"

"Well."

Was she playing coy or merely trying to think of a polite way to turn him down? His shivering limbs needed an answer. So did his heart.

She dropped to the sand beside him. *"Oui! Mais oui!"*

He rose and slipped the ring from his pocket. Rather than place it on her finger, he turned up her palm and set it there, wrapping her fingers around it.

Amalie glanced up at him, confused. He kissed away the look and smiled. "Grant me one thing, sweetheart," he said. "I want to do this right and proper. Before you put that ring on your finger, let me ask your father for your hand."

"Oh, Rob, yes, of course."

He pulled the ribbon from her hair and watched the dark locks blow free in the crisp breeze. Stringing the ring in the ribbon, he tied a knot and slipped the makeshift necklace over Amalie's head.

"Only the Lord knows when you will be free to put that

ring on your finger, but I want you to know something."

"What's that?" she asked, her lower lip trembling.

"In my heart we will never be apart. No matter what."

"No matter what."

Amalie fell into his embrace and stayed there until he led her to the truck. Once he helped her inside and closed the door, he walked toward the back of the truck.

Just out of sight of his passenger, he dropped to his knees behind the truck. "Thank You, Lord," he said softly. "Now that I have Amalie, You can send all Your blessings her way. She's all I need."

As he settled behind the wheel and cranked first the engine then the heater, Rob turned to Amalie. "I want to know one thing."

"What's that?"

"Why did you turn down the part?"

"That's easy," she said as she fingered the ribbon at her neck. "I realized the dreams I had been dreaming were the wrong ones." Amalie reached over to place her hand on Rob's arm. "Sometimes the Lord has to give you what you want so you can see it's not what you need."

"Amalie Breaux, that is profound."

With a shake of her head she turned her attention to the rolling waves on the beach below. "No, it's just the truth."

"Yes, it is, but what made you so certain that acting in the movies wasn't for you after all?"

Amalie turned her brown eyes in his direction and gave him an expression so solemn he half-expected her to call off the engagement. "It was something you said when you prayed for me."

"Oh? What was that?"

"The same thing the Lord's been whispering in my ear since I got here." She closed her eyes. "Perfect love casts out fear."

Rob swallowed hard and swiped at the irritating tears

gathering in the corner of his eyes. "He's been telling me the same thing since I met you, sweetheart. Think maybe we're meant to be?"

She snuggled up against him for the ride home. "You just might be right."

&

One more kiss and Rob turned the truck toward Franklin Street. Amalie held the ring in her hand for a moment longer then tucked it inside her bodice. The metal felt cold and heavy, but the promise it held caused her heart to soar.

"Amalie, I know we had intended to visit your parents at Christmas, but I'd like to propose a different plan." He paused to give her a sideways glance then signaled to turn onto Franklin Street. "I'll buy a train ticket this afternoon. Can you be ready to travel on Friday?"

"This Friday?"

He nodded. "I'll follow in a few weeks, say a day or two before Christmas. I think it's important that you and your family have some time together before I show up, don't you?"

"I suppose so," she said slowly, "but I'll miss you terribly."

Rob pulled the truck to a stop at the curb outside her apartment. "Every day without you will be torture, Amalie," he said as he brought her fingers to his lips. "But I don't know another way to do this."

Amalie thought a moment then nodded. "You're right. The prodigal has to return before the prince arrives."

Kissing her on the cheek, he chuckled. "You are priceless."

She sat back. "Say, shouldn't we tell your folks before I leave?"

"Sweetheart, as much as I want to spill the beans about our engagement, I think it would only be right to get your father's blessing before we say anything."

Wonderful. The rest of my life depends on what Papa approves of—again. But maybe it's best.

ॐ

Friday, December 5

Amalie followed Rob through the North Hollywood Rail Terminal, weaving with him through a crowd dotted with uniformed men and sobbing families. She tried not to listen as she heard one after the other tell their mothers, children, and wives they would see them soon. In a moment Rob would be saying the same to her.

While her future husband wasn't mustering with the troops, he was chafing at the bit to fly planes for his country. It didn't take a genius to know that if the war came, he would be gone.

Worse, she understood completely and could find no fault in his loyalty and patriotism. It made him who he was.

Rob wrapped his arm around her waist and drew her into an embrace. "Mother's going to see to it that your things are moved up to the house until you can come back to retrieve them."

"Was she suspicious?"

Rob grinned. "Mother's always suspicious, but she's been told the truth. You're taking some time to reunite with your family. There's no need in paying for an apartment if you're not living in it for a month or more." He paused. "To be honest, Mother was relieved. She said she prayed for you constantly, living where you did."

"If only she'd known me when I lived at the hotel." Amalie rested her head on Rob's shoulder. "That seems so long ago."

"It does, doesn't it?"

"All aboard," the conductor called, and the mass of passengers began to move past them.

Panic seized Amalie's heart, and she clung to Rob. "I can't go. I just can't. Please, go tell the conductor I need my bags."

Rob escorted her to a quiet corner. "Enough of that," he said softly. "We'll be together soon enough."

A pair of women wearing USO armbands strolled past. The reminder of war made Amalie shiver.

"No, Rob, please," she said. "Don't make me go."

He tugged on the ribbon at her neck and lifted it over her head. "I brought you a little something," he said. "Something a bit more sturdy than a hair ribbon." He strung the ring onto a chain and placed it around her neck. Lifting the ring to his lips, he kissed it then her. "That will have to do until Christmas, sweetheart," he said.

"Oh, Rob. . ." Further words were choked by the knot in her throat.

Rob led her to the train and placed his hands on her waist to lift her onto the steps. Once again she leaned into his arms.

"Don't make me leave you, Rob," she said through the tears. "I have this terrible feeling I won't ever see you again."

He straightened his spine and addressed her like an errant child. "You will get on the train, Amalie Breaux, and you will go home to make things right with your father and your mother. When I come to claim my bride, I don't want anything standing in my way. Do you understand?"

She nodded weakly.

"Then scoot."

"One more kiss?"

He complied, joining her on the steps to give her a kiss that felt as if it would last a lifetime. Or at least until Christmas.

"Wait," she called as he turned to step back onto the platform. "May I use your pocket knife?" Amalie asked quickly.

Puzzled, Rob nodded and handed the knife to her.

Amalie took the ribbon from Rob and cut it, then tied half to his wrist. "Let's just see how many ladies you pick up wearing a hair ribbon." She smiled as she gave back the knife.

He grinned and kissed her again, outdoing his previous performance and sending her scurrying into the train car dizzy. As she took her place by the window, she saw him searching for her.

Tugging and pulling, she finally managed to lower the glass. "Over here, darling!" she called and waved to him.

Rob hurried to the window and reached to touch her outstretched fingers. Just as they made contact the train's horn sounded, and the great steel wheels began to turn. Rob jogged alongside the train until it cleared the station.

"I love you," was the last thing she heard him say before the locomotive's whistle sounded and the train rolled around the bend.

"I love you, too, Rob," she whispered, thankful he had secured a private compartment for her.

The other half of the ribbon still in her hand, Amalie settled back for a good cry and a two-day ride. Suddenly her insistence that her quilt and pillow be with her on the train didn't seem so childish.

At some point she placed the ribbon in her Bible, carefully choosing 1 John 4:18 as the spot to mark.

"There is no fear in love; but perfect love casteth out fear: because fear hath torment," was the last thing she read before falling asleep wrapped in Mama's quilt and dreaming of Rob Tratelli.

twenty-two

Amalie awoke before the train stopped, as dawn broke over Louisiana. In addition to the letter she'd written, Rob had seen that a telegram was dispatched to inform the family of her arrival time. The odds were the telegram would reach them well before the letter. Just in case, she'd left him the telephone number of her brother-in-law's medical office. Of all the family members, Jeff Villare was the only one with a telephone.

She took particular care with her grooming that morning, washing up as best she could in the small basin-style facilities. The last thing she did was tuck the gold chain containing her engagement ring beneath her blouse. As she adjusted her collar, the train began to brake.

Heart pounding, Amalie leaned toward the window to search for someone, anyone, she knew. Her hopes plummeted when she saw no one she recognized standing on the platform.

"It's what I deserve," she whispered, folding the quilt and slipping it into her pillowcase. "I walked out of Latagnier, and I'll walk back in."

She lingered a moment in her compartment, choosing to let those in a hurry to depart do so. Finally, as the conductor made his last rounds, she gathered up her belongings and stepped into the narrow corridor.

Up ahead, sunlight blazed into the empty space where the open door awaited. She walked toward it then turned to step out into the Louisiana morning.

And there stood her papa.

Amalie paused a moment—froze, really—and dropped her pillowcase and handbag. And then she ran to him, with no question as to whether he would accept his wandering girl back.

His open arms reached for her and held her tight, lifting her feet off the ground then whirling her around in a circle. Her name became a laugh and then a sob.

She was home.

"Oh, Papa, I'm so sorry. Please forgive me."

"*C'est fini, ma fille.*" It is finished. "*Allons, bebe.*" Let's go home.

Somewhere behind her, Amalie became aware of a porter delivering her trunk and then of her father leading her out of the station toward the street. They rode in silence, jolting and bouncing over familiar rutted roads until Papa turned the truck into the long tree-covered driveway.

He stopped then, turning to face her with an expression very much like the one she'd left four months ago. "You did wrong, girl," he said gruffly, a quavering in his voice. "But I love you, and so does your mama."

"I love you, too, Papa," she somehow managed to say. "And I'm so sorry. I should never have left. I was wrong. I disobeyed you and God, and I feel awful."

Papa held up his hand to silence her. "We've said all we need to say about that, you hear?" When she nodded, he continued. "You're my baby girl, and nothing's gonna change that."

"Yes, Papa."

"Your mama and your sisters, they've been cooking for two days now. And your brothers, why, they've even been nice to one another." He grinned. "We've got a celebration planned for tonight. You still like your mama's gumbo, or did you get big-city tastes while you were gone?"

"Oh, yes, sir, I believe I'd welcome a bowl of Mama's gumbo."

That settled, Papa pressed on the gas and drove the truck toward the house. And like the prodigal in the Bible, Amalie returned home to a celebration.

That afternoon, after eating her fill of gumbo and rice with a second helping of sweet potato pie, Amalie curled up beside her sister Angeline on the sofa. The adults had gathered there to listen to the radio program while the little ones napped.

As the program began, Amalie's eyes felt heavy. "I believe I'm going to climb into bed with one of the babies," she said. "I need a nap."

"You go on ahead, *bebe*," Mama said. "I thought we might all go to town later. You want to ride along?"

"Of course," she said.

Glenn Miller's orchestra played as Amalie stood and headed down the hall. Suddenly the music stopped, and silence reigned.

"Theo, check to see if the radio's broken again," she heard Mama say.

"There's nothing wrong with it, honey," Papa replied. "See, the lights are on. Looks like somebody's cut into the broadcast to—"

"The Japanese have bombed Pearl Harbor!" the announcer shouted. "We are at war!"

❧

Monday, December 8
Hollywood, California

A day that will live in infamy. Rob listened to the words along with most of America, although he heard them as his truck was bouncing down the canyon road toward the city. His time had come, and though his heart broke, he must go and serve.

An image of Amalie's face swam before him, and he swiped at the tears. If only he could speak to her one last time before he left.

But what would he say? That he would be fine? To keep planning that springtime wedding?

All he could tell her was he loved her and that someday, if God allowed, he would come home to her. He'd said all that in the letter.

Besides, if he heard her voice or held her. . .

"Enough."

Rob left his truck at the curb with the keys in it and squared his shoulders before joining the long line outside the recruiting office. In his pocket were two letters, one to his folks and the other to Amalie. He'd mail them both from wherever they sent him.

As his turn came, Rob stepped up to the harried clerk and shook his hand. "Roberto Tratelli III, sir," he said. "I'm a pilot. I believe I might be of use to my country."

&

Tuesday, December 23
Latagnier, Louisiana

Amalie held the unopened letter against her chest and tried to slow the tears coursing down her cheeks. The postmark alone told her the tale. Rob, *her* Rob, had enlisted.

The letter, when she finally opened it, told her what she expected. He also begged her understanding and forgiveness that the news could not be delivered in person. And he pledged his love and vowed to return someday and put the ring on her finger.

He asked for prayers as well, but he needn't have bothered. Amalie had begun praying for Rob well before she finished the letter.

twenty-three

Amalie sat beside the bayou, a letter in her lap. She hadn't heard from Rob for nigh on three weeks, and her heart hurt with the possible reasons why. Before now he'd been prompt in writing almost every day. Sometimes the letters arrived in bunches, and other times they straggled in one or two at a time. Always they bore a military postmark and little information as to his whereabouts.

All she knew was that Rob was somewhere in the Pacific, flying missions that were too classified to mention. He ended each letter with a promise to return and an admonishment for her not to fear. He signed the letters pledging his love, and always beneath his scrawling signature he wrote 1 John 4:18.

Perfect love casts out fear.

On more than one occasion over the past three weeks, fear *had* gotten the better of her. A week ago Friday she'd been in the middle of caring for the babies at the defense factory, her new part-time job, when she was struck with the awful thought that something had happened to Rob.

She shook it off, of course, partly because the baby in her care chose to require a diaper change at that moment and partly because she held a firm belief that the Lord of the universe would never be so cruel as to take Rob away forever.

This letter was from Charlotte Tratelli, the woman who, if not for this awful war, would most likely be her mother-in-law by now. She'd received a letter or two every week from

Rob's mother, most of which contained chatty discussions of her work with different war efforts in the Los Angeles area.

"Don't be silly, girl," she said as she unfolded the elegant parchment and began to read. "It's just a letter. Not the end of the world."

As on past occasions Mrs. Tratelli used the first paragraph to inquire into Amalie's health and that of her family. She went on in the second paragraph to state how much she and Mr. Tratelli missed Amalie and wished her well and what war relief activities the pair had undertaken over the past week. That was normal.

Still the foreboding continued, a by-product of the feeling she'd been unable to shake all week.

With one paragraph left in the letter, Amalie let the paper drop into her lap. It was a fine spring afternoon, a day too lovely to think of anything but the Lord and His magnificent creation.

"You're stalling," she whispered. "Just get it over with, and you'll feel better."

With care she picked up the page and allowed her gaze to land on the last paragraph. Words jumped out of her.

I fear to tell you that a telegram came.
Our Rob has gone missing.
Shot down over the Pacific.
No evidence of his plane.

She saw him then, her Rob all dressed up in the fancy uniform of a flier. He stood next to an airplane proudly dubbed the *Amalie Breaux*. That picture had been her belated Christmas present, and it sat in a frame beside her bed even now.

Our Rob.
Missing.
No evidence of his plane.

Amalie let out a wail, and then the world went black.

⠮

Tuesday, August 25
New Iberia, Louisiana

Nights were the worst. Most days Amalie could put one foot in front of the other and get along without thinking. Sometimes, when a young mother would drop off a squirming toddler before taking her place on the assembly line, Amalie couldn't help crying, thinking of what might have been.

By now she might have had a baby of her own.

If not for the war.

The ring she wore around her neck would be solidly on her finger, and the man who gave it to her would be at her side.

If not for the war.

Amalie kept his letters in a box by her bed and his picture on her dresser. She'd found it was better to ease into seeing Rob. Awaking to his face hurt so much that the pain made getting out of bed difficult.

She'd been working full-time at the factory in New Iberia since early May, a fact that was hard to comprehend. Some days it felt like an eternity, and others it seemed like only yesterday she had walked into her boss's office.

Asking for an increase in work hours had been almost more than Amalie could bear. To admit she needed full-time employment meant admitting Rob would not be returning for her anytime soon. Still, she was a grown woman who needed to take care of herself. Helping out at the defense plant made her feel as if she was helping the war effort in some small way. She was thankful Mama and Papa were agreeable to her change in residence.

Within a few days Amalie had not only found the work she sought, but she'd also secured a room with two other plant workers at the boardinghouse across the street from the Evangeline Theater. Both were married women with husbands off fighting the war, and neither cared to talk about their worries.

That was fine by her.

Unlike Betty who had a pair of babies being taken care of by her mother and Ruby who spent endless hours writing to a sister in Houma whose husband hadn't been heard from since three days after the war began, Amalie rarely left the city. Going home became a place where she was forced to hide the ring she wore around her neck.

A ring she longed to slip onto her left hand.

She didn't, of course. She would leave that to Rob.

Some days she would peer out her window at the marquee and wonder what might have been, even when *Lady Sleuth* came to town with Vivian Leigh cast as Diandra.

Sure, it might be nice to see her name in lights but not at the expense of walking out of God's will. No, she might wish things were different, but never once did she wonder whether she had made the right choice.

&

Thursday, April 22, 1943
Latagnier, Louisiana

Her ride dropped Amalie and her suitcase off at the end of the driveway, leaving her with a long, cold walk back up to the house. That was fine by her. It matched her mood.

Tomorrow might be Good Friday, but tonight she felt anything but good.

Her mouth would be praising the Lord's resurrection in two days at Easter services, but Amalie had no doubt her heart would be elsewhere. It was a predicament, to be sure, relying on a God with whom she wasn't on the best of terms.

News of her loss had spread quickly, and folks had tended to give her wide berth. After all, there was no good way to express sorrow without admitting Rob was gone. The first few who tried hadn't been treated so well. Amalie soon tired of the apologies but never failed to give them.

Time had eased the memory of those closest to her, and Amalie suspected a few of them might even be conspiring to ease her pain by finding a substitute for Rob. The Dautrive fellow, ineligible for active duty due to his poor eyesight and faulty heart, certainly managed to come around regularly enough.

It was as if he had spies posted on the city limits who told him when she was headed home on her visits once or twice a month. No sooner did she arrive on Mama's doorstep than Tim Dautrive would show up right behind her.

"And there he is," she muttered as the house came into view. "Tim must have gotten a raise."

An unfamiliar car, low slung and dark in color, was parked next to Papa's Ford. Mama's fat orange cat sat atop the roof, surveying the horizon from a brand new vantage point.

She slowed her pace. Maybe she ought to head around to the back of the house, see to the eggs in the henhouse or check on what sort of weeding might need to be done in Mama's flower bed.

Anything to keep from having to face an evening making polite conversation with Tim Dautrive.

Unfortunately Mama spotted her and waved. Now she was stuck. She strolled toward her mother, who was emptying a basin of dishwater into the grass, and gave her a kiss on the cheek.

"*Bonsoir, bebe.*" Mama straightened and cut her gaze to the house then back at Amalie. "You're moving kind of slow today. If I didn't know better, I'd think you were putting off going inside."

Amalie shrugged. "Nonsense, Mama."

"Get on inside with you." Mama gave Amalie a light swat with her dishcloth. "I don't believe you'll be disappointed with your papa's choice of supper guests."

"I know, Mama. It's Tim Dautrive. I wish you would let me have some say in who I see, or rather if I want to see anyone at all."

Mama's grin broadened. "Oh, I think that can be arranged."

"I'm tired, Mama. Do I have to spend time with Tim? I'm going to be honest with you. There's no reason for me to spend time with him. Nothing is ever going to come of it. Nothing."

There. She'd spoken her piece. She'd have to say it all over again to Papa, but at least Mama now knew how she felt.

"Just go on inside and give the man a chance, will you?" Mama paused. "And no matter what wants to come out of your mouth, hold your tongue until the man's done talking. Promise me that."

"I promise, Mama, but as soon as he's done, I'm going to make my excuses. I don't have it in me tonight to socialize."

"All right, baby," Mama said.

Now that she'd been spotted, she need not tarry. Mama was watching.

Amalie climbed the stairs and set her bag on the porch. Papa's old hound dog sniffed the canvas bag then wagged his tail and offered her his nose.

"Its about time you woke up," she said as she ticked the canine's favorite spot behind his ears. "Some watchdog you are, letting the likes of that guy into the house." She pointed to the car for effect. "Next time you see that car coming up the drive, how about you chase him off, eh?"

"Amalie, that you?"

Papa's call wasn't easily ignored. "Yes, sir," she said.

"Come on in here. There's someone here to see you."

"Yes, Papa, I know. It's—"

Amalie stepped inside and stopped where she stood. The screen door might have hit her—she wasn't sure.

"Rob?"

twenty-four

"Rob?" Amalie found her feet but took a step and lost them once more. The room seemed to swim around her, and somehow Papa dragged a chair to her so she could sit.

Rob rose with difficulty, one leg stiff. He seemed to want to say something but remained silent. This had to be a dream. She'd had so many over the last months.

Amalie shook her head and pinched the inside of her wrist. When a vague sensation of pain radiated up her arm, she gave it heed.

"You're here. In Latagnier."

"Yes," he said softly, "I am. In fact I've been here almost a week. I had to take care of a few things before I felt able to come out here." He paused. "Before I could approach your papa."

"What?" The room tilted then quickly righted. Amalie fell back into the chair then looked over at Papa.

"This boy says you used to want to marry up with him. Is that so? You still want him for a husband?"

Her gaze drifted back to Rob who leaned heavily on the back of the chair beside her father. Reality set in, and so did the crying.

"Oh, yes, I do," she said through the tears. "I do."

Amalie flew into Rob's embrace then backed away when he groaned in pain. "I'm so sorry," she said.

He caught her in his arms and pulled her to him. "Do you know how long I've been waiting to do this? I drove past your father's driveway at least three times a day in the hopes I would see you. I wanted any excuse not to wait until my business was finished before I approached your father."

165

"You wouldn't have found me here," she said. "I've been working in New Iberia."

He nodded. "That's what your brother Ernest said."

"You've talked to my brother?"

Rob chuckled. "You might say I needed his help." At her questioning glance he shook his head. "I'll tell you all about it in good time. For now, I have something else to handle." He turned his attention to Papa who called loudly for Mama.

"Right here, Theo," she said. Of course she'd been listening from the hall. Mama was famous for that.

She took her place behind Papa's chair, one arm wrapped around his shoulder. Papa looked up at her then regarded Rob with an emotionless expression.

"State your business, young man."

"Yes, sir." He released his grasp on Amalie and turned his attention to Papa. "Sir, I know I've been away far longer than I'd like to think on, but I believe my love for your daughter has only grown stronger in my absence." He glanced at Amalie then looked back at Papa. "I'm prepared to take good care of Amalie, to love her and remain true to her the rest of my days. If you'll just say the words, I'll marry her on the spot."

Amalie held her breath while Papa considered the statement. She felt Rob reach for her hand and squeeze it, and she gave him a weak smile.

"Young man, you've served our country proud, and for that I respect you. You've also been man enough to come to me before you put a ring on my girl's finger. As you and I have already cleared up a few questions I had, I'm going to say that you have my permission to marry up with my Amalie."

Rob let out a whoop, and Amalie's tears returned.

"Hold on now. I'm not done." He pointed at Rob. "While I said you could marry up with her, I did not tell you it was all right to marry up on the spot. I'll expect a dignified courtship and a church wedding."

Rob reached to shake Papa's hand. "Sir, I agree to your terms."

"I don't," Amalie said.

"What's this?" Rob said. "What's wrong?"

Amalie linked arms with Rob. "Oh, I like the church wedding part, but I don't believe a dignified courtship is necessary." She looked into Rob's eyes and blinked hard to still the tears. "How soon can we put on a wedding? I think we've waited long enough."

"The girl's right, Theo. How about I talk to the parson after Good Friday services and see if I can't get us a date on the church calendar?" Mama looked at Papa. "As soon as possible, don't you think?"

Papa's expression remained thoughtful before he finally broke into a grin. "I believe that sounds fine. Welcome to the family, son."

"Thank you, sir." Rob smiled. "With your permission, Mr. Breaux, I'd like to make our engagement official."

❧

Dropping to one knee with more pain than he cared to admit or show, Rob looked up into the eyes of the woman whose memory had kept him alive during dark days.

She was crying again. If he had the strength and the ability, he would have reached for his handkerchief. As it was, remaining in this position took everything he had.

"Amalie Breaux," he said in a voice that trembled too much to suit him. "*Amalie, vous m'épouserez?* Will you do me the honor of being my wife?"

Her "yes" seemed to float toward him on angels' wings as he fell to the floor.

A moment later Amalie sank down beside him and settled in his arms.

"You need some help up, son?" Mr. Breaux asked.

"No, sir. I believe I'll just sit here a spell, though."

Mr. Breaux nodded and rose to lead his wife from the

room. "Come now, Cleo. Let's give the children some time to themselves."

Amalie grasped Rob's face with both hands and shook her head. "It's you. It's really you," she said. "Not a dream. You."

"Yes, it's me." He rose and winced at the pain shooting up his leg. The doctors told him it would take awhile to mend his body. His heart, however, had repaired itself immediately upon catching sight of Amalie Breaux.

"There's so much I want to tell you, Amalie."

"We have a lifetime for that."

He nodded. "I want to show you what I've been doing this week."

She gave him a mock frown. "Yes, I'd like to see what was more important than seeing me."

Rob gathered her tighter into his embrace. "*Nothing* was more important than seeing you. But I had to prove to myself and to your papa that I could take care of you." He paused. "Now give me a minute to get back on my feet."

The minute stretched a little longer, and it was nearing a half-hour later when they climbed into Rob's vehicle. A short while afterward he turned onto Old Shell Road and pulled the car to a stop outside Ziggy Labauve's barn.

Rob got out and, despite his stiff leg, walked around to open Amalie's door before she could do it herself. "Come on," he said. "I'm anxious to show you this." He paused to grasp her wrist. "Sweetheart, in all the excitement, I forgot to ask if you still have the ring I gave you the first time I asked you to marry me."

She lifted the chain from its place beneath her blouse and handed the ring to Rob. Removing it from the chain, he placed the ring on her finger.

"Now it's official," he said softly.

"Not until we seal it with a kiss."

"Absolutely." He gave her a kiss then quickly took a step

back. "Let's go see what's inside the barn."

Amalie followed him as he headed for the big double doors. Opening them revealed a small airplane. A crop duster.

"Rob, what's this?"

He grinned and joined her beside the plane. "The beginning of my empire, I hope."

"What?"

"It's like this. Before I left for the war, Uncle Gio and I were trying to decide whether to sign the contracts on the office and hangar space, remember?"

"Yes."

"Well, once war broke out, I knew what I had to do. Uncle Gio agreed, and we let that opportunity slip by. I always had it in my mind that I would find another way to make a living out of flying." He paused and swallowed the lump in his throat before continuing. "I've had plenty of time to think about what the Lord wants me to do, and I believe this is it."

"I don't understand."

"Honey, I bought this land from Mr. Labauve. It comes with a barn for my plane and a little house over beyond the ridge. I want to build a life here, Amalie. I want our home to be over there under that stand of trees, and I want to raise our babies here." Again he was forced to pause. "What do you think of that, sweetheart?"

"So you're saying you want to live here? In Latagnier?"

"Well, most of the time anyway. We'd have to take the kids to California to see their grandparents occasionally. In case you're worried, I've already talked to Mother and Pop, and they are thrilled. Now all that remains is to ask you what you think."

"Oh, Rob," she said softly. "I think it's a dream come true."

NANA'S BUTTERMILK CORNBREAD

1½ cups plus 2 teaspoons yellow cornmeal
¼ cup flour
1 teaspoon salt
1 teaspoon baking soda
2 cups buttermilk
1 egg
¼ cup oil

Preheat oven to 425 degrees. Pour oil into iron skillet and heat in oven. Mix together dry ingredients (reserving the 2 teaspoons cornmeal) then mix in 1 cup buttermilk and the egg. Blend in remaining cup of buttermilk. When oil is hot, pour it into batter and mix well. Sprinkle last 2 teaspoons cornmeal in bottom of skillet and put back into oven to brown for 2 minutes or until brown. Pour batter into hot skillet and let cook 20 minutes or until done and browned nicely on top. Serves 6–8.

A Letter To Our Readers

Dear Reader:

In order that we might better contribute to your reading enjoyment, we would appreciate your taking a few minutes to respond to the following questions. We welcome your comments and read each form and letter we receive. When completed, please return to the following:

Fiction Editor
Heartsong Presents
PO Box 719
Uhrichsville, Ohio 44683

1. Did you enjoy reading *Bayou Dreams* by Kathleen Miller Y'Barbo?
   ❏ Very much! I would like to see more books by this author!
   ❏ Moderately. I would have enjoyed it more if

   _____

   _____

   _____

2. Are you a member of **Heartsong Presents**? ❏ Yes ❏ No
   If no, where did you purchase this book? _____

   _____

3. How would you rate, on a scale from 1 (poor) to 5 (superior), the cover design? _____

4. On a scale from 1 (poor) to 10 (superior), please rate the following elements.

____	Heroine	____	Plot
____	Hero	____	Inspirational theme
____	Setting	____	Secondary characters

5. These characters were special because? _____

_____

_____

6. How has this book inspired your life? _____

_____

_____

7. What settings would you like to see covered in future
   Heartsong Presents books? _____

_____

_____

8. What are some inspirational themes you would like to see
   treated in future books? _____

_____

_____

9. Would you be interested in reading other **Heartsong
   Presents** titles? ❏ Yes ❏ No

10. Please check your age range:
    ❏ Under 18   ❏ 18-24
    ❏ 25-34   ❏ 35-45
    ❏ 46-55   ❏ Over 55

Name _____

Occupation _____

Address _____

City, State, Zip_____

BRIDES OF THE EMPIRE

4 stories in 1

Oppressed but not broken, three young women within the Roman Empire struggle to find true and lasting love. Titles include: *The Eagle and the Lamb*, *Edge of Destiny*, and *My Enemy, My Love* by author Darlene Mindrup.

Historical, paperback, 368 pages, 5³/₁₆" x 8"

_____

Please send me ____ copies of *Brides of the Empire*. I am enclosing $6.97 for each.
(Please add $2.00 to cover postage and handling per order. OH add 7% tax.)

Send check or money order, no cash or C.O.D.s, please.

Name_____

Address _____

City, State, Zip _____

To place a credit card order, call 1-740-922-7280.
Send to: Heartsong Presents Readers' Service, PO Box 721, Uhrichsville, OH 44683

Heart♥ong

Presents

__HP576 *Letters from the Enemy*, S. M. Warren
__HP579 *Grace*, L. Ford
__HP580 *Land of Promise*, C. Cox
__HP583 *Ramshackle Rose*, C. M. Hake
__HP584 *His Brother's Castoff*, L. N. Dooley
__HP587 *Lilly's Dream*, P. Darty
__HP588 *Torey's Prayer*, T. V. Bateman
__HP591 *Eliza*, M. Colvin
__HP592 *Refining Fire*, C. Cox
__HP595 *Surrendered Heart*, J. Odell
__HP596 *Kiowa Husband*, D. Mills
__HP599 *Double Deception*, L. Nelson Dooley
__HP600 *The Restoration*, C. M. Hake
__HP603 *A Whale of a Marriage*, D. Hunt
__HP604 *Irene*, I. Ford
__HP607 *Protecting Amy*, S. P. Davis
__HP608 *The Engagement*, K. Comeaux
__HP611 *Faithful Traitor*, J. Stengl
__HP612 *Michaela's Choice*, L. Harris
__HP615 *Gerda's Lawman*, L. N. Dooley
__HP616 *The Lady and the Cad*, T. H. Murray
__HP619 *Everlasting Hope*, T. V. Bateman
__HP620 *Basket of Secrets*, D. Hunt
__HP623 *A Place Called Home*, J. L. Barton
__HP624 *One Chance in a Million*, C. M. Hake
__HP627 *He Loves Me, He Loves Me Not*,
          R. Druten
__HP628 *Silent Heart*, B. Youree
__HP631 *Second Chance*, T. V. Bateman

__HP632 *Road to Forgiveness*, C. Cox
__HP635 *Hogtied*, L. A. Coleman
__HP636 *Renegade Husband*, D. Mills
__HP639 *Love's Denial*, T. H. Murray
__HP640 *Taking a Chance*, K. E. Hake
__HP643 *Escape to Sanctuary*, M. J. Conner
__HP644 *Making Amends*, J. L. Barton
__HP647 *Remember Me*, K. Comeaux
__HP648 *Last Chance*, C. M. Hake
__HP651 *Against the Tide*, R. Druten
__HP652 *A Love So Tender*, T. V. Batman
__HP655 *The Way Home*, M. Chapman
__HP656 *Pirate's Prize*, L. N. Dooley
__HP659 *Bayou Beginnings*, K. Y'Barbo
__HP660 *Hearts Twice Met*, Freda Chrisman
__HP663 *Journeys*, T. H. Murray
__HP664 *Chance Adventure*, K. E. Hake
__HP667 *Sagebrush Christmas*, B. L. Etchison
__HP668 *Duel Love*, B. Youree
__HP671 *Sooner or Later*, V. McDonough
__HP672 *Chance of a Lifetime*, K. E. Hake
__HP672 *Bayou Secrets*, K. Y'Barbo
__HP672 *Beside Still Waters*, T. V. Bateman
__HP679 *Rose Kelly*, J. Spaeth
__HP680 *Rebecca's Heart*, L. Harris
__HP683 *A Gentlemen's Kiss*, K. Comeaux
__HP684 *Copper Sunrise*, C. Cox
__HP687 *The Ruse*, T. H. Murray
__HP688 *A Handful of Flowers*, C. M. Hake

Great Inspirational Romance at a Great Price!

Heartsong Presents books are inspirational romances in contemporary and historical settings, designed to give you an enjoyable, spirit-lifting reading experience. You can choose wonderfully written titles from some of today's best authors like Peggy Darty, Sally Laity, DiAnn Mills, Colleen L. Reece, Debra White Smith, and many others.

When ordering quantities less than twelve, above titles are $2.97 each.
Not all titles may be available at time of order.

SEND TO: **Heartsong Presents** Reader's Service
               P.O. Box 721, Uhrichsville, Ohio 44683
Please send me the items checked above. I am enclosing $ _____
(please add $2.00 to cover postage per order. OH add 7% tax. NJ
add 6%). Send check or money order, no cash or C.O.D.s, please.
        To place a credit card order, call 1-740-922-7280.

NAME _____

ADDRESS _____

CITY/STATE _____ ZIP_____

HPS 5-06